DEAD OR ALIVE

Dean Carson

Dean Carson has asserted his right under the Copyright, Design and Patents Act, 1988, to be identified as the author of this work.

First published 2015 by Endeavour Press Ltd.

Printed and bound in Great Britain by Clays Ltd, St Ives plc

ISBN: 978-1-911445-10-4

First published 2015 by Endeavour Press Ltd.

Printed and bound in Great Britain by Clays Ltd, St Ives plc.

Endeavour Press is the UK's leading independent publisher.

We publish a wide range of genres including history, crime, romance, historical fiction and thrillers.

Every week, we give away free e-books.

For more information about our titles, go to our website:
www.endeavourpress.com/our-books/

Or sign up for our newsletter at:
www.endeavourpress.com

Table of Contents

ONE

Mostar, Bosnia & Herzegovina

The stone glistened in the pale sunlight like little diamonds. Microscopic shards of schist caught the light and sprinkled it back at me. The rain a few minutes earlier had brought out the beauty of the stones, though stones have a beauty of their own even when dry. About one in fifteen of the rocks were schist; the rest were tenelija, a local limestone. Every time my hammer struck one on the wall surrounding the small park it rang with a strange hollow sound. This intrigued me. The rocks were not hollow. My hammer was not hollow. Where did the sound come from? Just one more mystery of the mason's art.

When I hit the concrete between the rocks it sounded dull but right. That was the sound I expected. And that was where I was striking most of the time. I was pointing the wall. Pointing is what we stonemasons call the fiddly bits between the stones. Do it right, and the wall looks great. Do it wrong, and it's an untidy mess.

Actually, I am not a stonemason. I am more of a bounty hunter. Not the regular bail bond chaser – more of an old-fashioned bag 'em and tag 'em bounty hunter. My job is to track down people who don't want to be tracked down and kill them for a price. So I wasn't really pointing the wall. I was staking out the warehouse across the river Neretva, in the old town of Mostar. I was about two hundred metres up river from the famous Stari Most, or Old Bridge, one of the gems of Islamic architecture in Central Europe. The bridge was bombed into the middle of next year during the war in the nineties – I can't remember when or exactly why. But the new bridge, with its high stone arch, was a worthy replacement.

I had been working on the wall for four days and, even though I am no stonemason, I was happy with my progress. And no one had questioned what I was doing there. Dusty face and hair, old clothes bought in a second-hand shop in Sarajevo and a grumpy attitude had been the perfect cover. I don't speak Serbian, but I do speak drunk and homeless. Anyone who looked like striking up a conversation with me got the same re-action; a crazed stare, incoherent muttering and a spit-speckled curse. It was enough. They quickly got the message and left me in peace. Four days of hammering, tapping and pointing.

Four days of watching the warehouse, thirty metres from me, but separated by the deep gorge of the river.

My target wasn't due until today. I knew that, but if I had arrived today I would have been spotted. Four days were need-ed to build my cover. Now I was just some old man doing a menial job. I was invisible. I kept tapping away.

Jarko Radoslav was my target. He had been one of the leaders of the Croat faction during the conflict in the nineties, charged in his absence with war crimes and crimes against hu-manity. He wasn't one of the big guys and there was no politi-cal pressure to bring him to justice. But someone in the Justice Department, or the Pentagon, had decided he was going to be another casualty in the war on terror. I had picked up the contract. There was a price tag of $40,000 on his head and I was going to collect.

I have rules. The world has to be a better place without my target. I have no problem killing women, but they have to deserve it. Kids are not on the menu. No kid is ever so bad that they need to suffer the ultimate sanction. And no collateral damage, ever. That's the golden rule, the one I have never broken. So I couldn't just put a bomb in the warehouse and let nature take its course. I had to do this job myself.

It was three o'clock when the dark Merc with the blacked-out windows pulled up at the gate of the warehouse. A man as big as a garden shed got out and came into the yard. He looked all around. He even looked directly at me. Then I saw his head bend as he spoke into a small microphone dangling from the earpiece he wore. Whatever he said, it must have been all right because the car slowly advanced down the side of the warehouse and pulled to a stop at the low wall facing the river. A second man got out, almost as big as the first. He was the driver. He opened the rear door of the car and a dapper figure in his early fifties emerged. He was small and slim, and even from my vantage point I could see the suit was expensive.

Now? Perhaps. Then the side door of the warehouse opened and two men stepped out. The men he had come to meet; the guys with the heroin. Radoslav stepped forward and shook hands with one of the men. Then they turned to walk into the warehouse. It had to be now – I might not get the chance again.

I glanced into my rough wooden toolbox. The long-barrelled sports pistol was inside, the silencer securely screwed into place. A thin wire led from the trigger of the pistol to a small black box. It was a remote control switch and vital to the plan. Quickly but calmly I took the gun and raised it to shoulder height, extending my arm out straight. None of them were looking in my direction. Thirty-five metres – an easy shot. The pistol only shot a .22 but I had a clear bead on his temple. One shot should do it. If I was off a fraction and he survived his brain would be so fucked up it wouldn't make much difference. I could still collect my fee.

He was at the door now. I stilled my breath, then slowly squeezed the trigger. Two things happened at once. There was a gentle "phut" from my gun but no flash, no tell-tale expulsion of smoke or gas. The suppressor dealt with that. And there was a deafening explosion from the other side of the river. The remote control had guaranteed that. The explosion was accompanied by a puff of smoke from the explosive charge, a standard disco flash pot.

Both bodyguards immediately turned towards the noise, drawing their guns and crouching low, as their boss stumbled and fell clumsily to the ground. They had their backs to me. I had plenty of time. It would have been a matter of two seconds to put a slug in the backs of both their heads. But that wasn't the brief. The slime who was selling the heroin wasn't part of the brief either. No collateral damage. I casually lowered my hand, dropped the gun into my toolbox, closed it, then began to walk slowly away. Job done. Another forty big ones in the bank.

TWO

I ditched the gun on the other side of the bridge, a couple of hundred metres from the warehouse. It was easy. Lots of people were milling around, but I went down to the water's edge and began throwing scraps of bread to the ducks. In the feathered flurry it was easy to toss the gun into a dark and deep spot. One duck dove for it, but came up disappointed.

The remote control (which came from a child's toy car) ended up in a bin near the main bus station, about five minutes' walk from the old quarter. I ended up in the toilet of the station. When I emerged ten minutes later I was in jeans and a leather jacket. I had a heavy rucksack on my back and I looked like any other hippie, except I was a few years older, and a bit more respectable. I was wearing thick old-fashioned glasses to give me a professorial air. The glasses were genius. From the outside they bulged my eyes, giving me the look of a myopic owl. But from my side they were just plain glass. My eyesight is perfect, twenty-twenty.

There was lots of dust in my hair from the masonry work, which added a decade to my age. If I was a vain man that would have been a problem. But it was a good look for a man trying to get away with murder.

I ambled slowly back to the historic quarter. Sirens blared in the distance, but there was no noticeable stirring in the air. I suppose the people of this blighted city are used to mayhem, and one more man in a suit biting the dust was not news. I took my time, because tourists walk slowly. I looked in every shop window and stopped and admired a gallery display. Partly this was to check reflections to see I wasn't being followed. Partly it was to blend in. And partly it was because this was my first – and probably last – time in Mostar, and now that I was finished working I wanted to enjoy it.

The damage from the war in the nineties has been cleaned up beautifully and the place was full of medieval stone buildings and narrow streets and lanes. I was tempted to stop for a coffee but sense prevailed and I turned towards the Hostel Anya, where I was loosely based. Casually I scanned the faces I passed. A mix of old Europe and modern tourist. Then I spotted her – a flash of auburn curls in the mid-distance. Being a bit of an expert in surveillance, I was able to scope her out without spinning my head like a horny teenager. I liked what I saw.

She was in her late twenties, maybe touching thirty, slim and athletic. Her eyes were the soft brown of autumnal leaves and her hair continued the autumnal theme, auburn flecked with copper. She was tall – or maybe that was the long legs – and carrying a backpack, so she was a tourist like me. Was she on her own? I wasn't interested. Being a bounty hunter plays havoc with relationships. But I am a man, and men play the odds. She was hot. Not in an obvious way, but in the sort of way that on second glance might make a bishop rethink his vows. So I smiled as I passed and chanced a Hello.

She frowned at me, then snapped: "Not interested. I don't

have daddy issues."

Ouch. I grinned and moved on. Once again the odds had let me down.

When I reached the hostel Zloti, the concierge (and owner, I guess) grinned and stood.

"Mr Wilson, welcome back to my hostel of humbleness."

Wilson – that was my name for this mission. Mark Wilson, in tribute to an American magician.

Zloti spoke English like a native, but a native of no country I was familiar with.

"Thanks – my stuff still safe?" I asked.

I had left the humble hostel a week ago, ostensibly to hike in the surrounding mountains, and he was holding on to a big suitcase for me. He took it out of a back room and I signed for a room for the night.

"I'll be checking out in the morning," I told him.

"Is no problemo," he assured me.

Reassured, I went up to my second floor room and had a shower. Ten years came off with the dust. Daddy issues, I thought. You don't know what you're missing.

As I towelled off I clicked on the kettle. I threw the window open as wide as it would go, letting the warm breeze waft through. Outside, the birds twittered. From upstairs, I could hear the tinny strains of Beyoncé. Kids these days – no taste in music.

It took a minute for the laptop to fire up, then I connected it to my smartphone. The smartphone is actually a satellite phone and rather smarter than the average. It provides a very secure and fast internet hook-up that doesn't reveal my location. That can be important in my line of work. Sipping an instant coffee, I logged on.

The first site I went to was (try to forget this ...) The Magic Bistro. It's great – full of geeks discussing magic. But, unknown to them, there is a secret side to the Bistro. It's called the dark internet. A dedicated community of bounty hunters, professional hit men and mercenaries mingle there with the sort of shady characters who use our services. We log on and we are invisible to the magicians. But if someone disturbs us or tries to trace our online history, they find discussions of new card tricks and how to take care of your rabbit.

I clicked on to the buy and sell forum. This is the heart of the Bistro, a marketplace for people with a very peculiar set of skills. People like me. Scrolling down, I found what I was looking for: an auction for a second-hand arm chop illusion. The seller was based in Bosnia. Reading between the lines, that meant someone was looking to put out a contract on some geezer in Bosnia. I had expressed my interest in owning the arm chopper. The deal had been done for forty dollars.

That might seem to be a low price for a man's life and an unsustainable economic proposition. But every number on the Bistro is a multiple of 1000. So I was going to be paid $40,000 for that afternoon's work. Obscene money, until you think about premiership footballers. And remember, I can only do so many of these jobs a year. It is not like sweeping chimneys.

I posted a breezy message on the forum: "Chopper arrived safely this afternoon. I am delighted with it." In case you are having difficulty translating: I had just told the man who had hired me – a CIA operative who liaises with the UN Security Council – that the target, Radoslav, was dead. That was his cue to wire the money to my Swiss bank account. Happy days.

I drained the coffee and turned my chair towards the window. The view was breathtaking. Beautiful cliffs of verdant foliage swept up from the gleaming sandstone of the ancient buildings. It was warm outside and the window faced away from the street, giving a measure of silence. I was at peace. Time to meditate. I find mindfulness keeps me focused, especially when the action gets hot. I took a deep breath and let my eyes close.

Then the phone pinged. I opened my eyes again and looked at the text. It was from my brother. The annoying brother. Actually, that is not true. I have only one brother. But he is still the annoying one.

The text read: "Your sister has decided to do a porn movie. What are you going to do about it?"

That raised an eyebrow. My sister, who is a good deal less annoying than my brother, is a classically trained dancer and last I heard had been working as a first artist in the corps de ballet on a major West End production of *Swan Lake*. I know the tutus can be short, but it was a long stretch to call this porn, even for my brother. He is a teacher, and the most virtuous man he knows. He sees everything we do as an affront to his dignity. I laughed inwardly at the "your sister" bit. Lester has always felt that Jane and I have a special relationship that he is excluded from. He is right; we like each other.

The text could wait. I was in the wind-down phase after a big job, and I was going to wind down, come hell or high water.

I took a deep breath and let my eyes close again. I began to focus on my breathing, following the breath in and out, letting it slow naturally. Thoughts came and went like butterflies fluttering in the summer air. I let them come and go, not following them, just observing them dispassionately. There were sounds from the outside, distant traffic. Some kid in a neighbouring room playing his music too loud. A girl screeching joyfully the way only girls can. A gentle vibration, repeated.

A gentle vibration ...

That thought stuck. I am good at this mindfulness. Thoughts drift by like twigs on a river. But this twig didn't drift by. It snagged on something. I didn't consciously register the thought. It all happened below the surface of my awareness. But suddenly I was on my feet. Before I had even started to reignite the mental processes I was half way across the room. From memory, I knew where the window was and I launched myself in a spectacular dive at the empty space.

A gentle vibration – someone's phone was ringing in my room. And it wasn't mine. I had put my phone in my pocket after disconnecting it from the laptop.

As I sailed through the window a second thought came crashing through my serene mindfulness: thank God it's open. And then a third thought pushed out the second: it's only a bloody phone. Why am I overreacting?

Next thing I knew I was in the air, my eyes open and

assessing my situation. It was not good. I had reacted instinctively. Had I put some thought into it I might have recalled that I was staying on the second floor. I might have looked in the room and found the phone that the previous guest had obviously left behind. I might have stepped out the door and walked down the stairs. Too late now. I looked down and could see the ground – a concrete patio – ten metres below me. I have a high opinion of myself, but I'm no Superman. Gravity is one of the few laws you can't break and this was not going to end well. But fortune favours the brave and chance favours the prepared mind, and … there was a tree.

I hit the tree and began to fall through the branches, crashing towards the ground. I managed to straighten my body so that I hit the concrete feet first, crumpling like a paratrooper and rolling. I came to rest with my back against the tree and tucked my head into my chest. I brought my arms up over my head, closed my eyes and tried to press my shoulders into my ears.

All the time I was cursing my training. What sort of moron jumps out a window when a phone rings? The sort of moron who has been over-trained to such an extent that he reacts instinctively without thinking, his reflexes honed to such a fine edge that he begins to move before his brain kicks in, or even before his eyes open. I had punched out civilians who bumped into me on the underground and hidden under a counter in a perfume store when someone clicked a lighter. But never had I jumped out a window when a phone rang. Maybe I would have to rethink this mindfulness.

Then the air shattered and the noise of a thousand screaming demons filled my head, and the debris began raining down from the sky.

THREE

You got it in one – my instincts had trumped my brain.

The carriages in the train of thought filled in rapidly. The phone must have been connected to a sound activated switch. Probably an untraceable burner phone that someone rang as soon as I called in the successful hit. The switch was connected to a fuse, which was connected to the explosive. Simple. Except it had been planted by an amateur. A pro would have made sure that the phone was not set to vibrate before ringing. That mistake had given me two seconds, enough to leap out a window and hit a tree, which saved my life.

I took my arms off my head and stood, feeling shaky. I turned and looked around the tree trunk. Where my room had been there was a big hole in the side of the building and the floor above had fallen in on it. A cloud of dust rose into the air, but there was very little smoke and what was left of my room wasn't burning. That meant high explosive rather than incendiary. Whoever wanted me dead had not been afraid of overkill.

Then I heard the screaming, and all trains of thought pulled into the station. I had a choice; run for my life or stay and help. The best course of action was obvious. Someone was trying to kill me and I didn't know who he was or whether he was in the vicinity to finish the job. Despite this, I moved towards the wreckage of the building. I can be stupid that way.

The back door was open. Inside, the ground floor looked relatively undamaged. But it was strewn with wreckage from my room above and there was a gaping hole in the ceiling. The blast had set off a sprinkler system and water was cascading from the roof. A cloud of dust billowed down the stairs. Zloti was standing at the reception desk, slack-jawed. He had the vacant look of a cow before the milking parlour. I punched his shoulder hard enough to get his attention, then bellowed right in his face: "Phone the cops and ambulance. Then get the fuck out. The building might collapse."

He looked at me. I pointed towards the phone and he came alive, reaching for the receiver. Then I was up the stairs, trying to reach the screaming girl. The first eight steps were fine, but a pile of plaster and wood blocked the top flight and made progress impossible. There were long wooden joists and sheets of plasterboard but I couldn't see any bricks. The interior of the house was simple sheet rock construction and what I was looking at were not the remains of a supporting wall. Which meant I could move it.

Easy to say, not so easy to do. It took me several vital seconds to get one long bit of wood out of the way and when it moved all the plasterboard settled. But it left me a passage through to the top of the stairs and the corridor. I could see right through where my door – and my wall – should have been, through the wreckage of my room and out into the yard at the back and the verdant cliffs behind, through a shimmer of settling dust that looked like a heat haze. This could not be stable.

The floor of the corridor was still intact. It looked safe, but I clung to the wall furthest away from my room just in case. I followed the sound of the screaming and came to the room next to mine. I didn't need to knock. The door was hanging loosely in the mangled frame. I wrenched it out and tossed it aside, then entered the bedroom. It looked just like mine had once done and had the same open view of the cliffs – most of the view coming from the huge hole in the wall dividing it from my room. There was a girl sitting on the bed with earphones on, connected to the remains of what might once have been an iPod. Or a cheap knock-off, like mine. She was about twenty and as pale as moonlight on fresh snow. She was immobile, but her mouth was open and she was screaming.

Her right arm lay by her side, bent at an angle that evolution had never intended. Unless she was a circus worker with a double-jointed elbow, this was the source of her screams. She must have been in agony. From her elbow the arm stretched backwards in a bloody mess, resting along a cushion on the sofa. An ugly lump of masonry with jagged edges lay across the arm, touching her side. Blood had sprayed all over her t-shirt, but it wasn't spraying now. That was good. She wasn't going to bleed out.

She hadn't seen me come in. She hadn't noticed anything. She was just staring at where the wall once had been, wailing like a lost banshee. I am used to violence and its effects, but I am more used to the dead than the living in this condition. Her wailing was unsettling me. Every fibre of my being screamed at me to run, but I could not. Not now. She was in shock, and when the shock wore off it was only going to get worse.

I stood in front of her, blocking her view. But as she was just staring vacantly I wasn't really blocking anything. Her eyes were dead. I needed to get her moving. She couldn't stay here. Even if the emergency services were on their way the room might not be stable. So I did the only thing I could think of. I drew my hand back and slapped her across the face, hard. She blinked, then turned and took in my face.

"My arm," she whispered.

I bent and grabbed the lump of masonry. It weighed several kilos, but I work out and I throw several kilos about the gym for breakfast. I yanked hard and it came off her arm. I rolled it on to the floor.

"Can you stand?"

I didn't wait for an answer. Taking her by her good arm and shoulder I lifted her off the sofa and began to cross the room. I was none too gentle but I figured she was in so much pain and shock a shove was not going to count in the grand scheme of things. And I might be saving her life. When we got out to the corridor I threw caution to the wind. To hell with hogging the wall – she didn't have the capacity to understand that right now. So I hurried her along to the top of the stairs and tried to manoeuvre her through the debris. Luckily Zloti was there, clearing the passage. He took my walking wounded and led her downstairs. I ran back up, determined to finish my sweep.

There were two more rooms on the second floor and both doors were closed. I tried the first and it was not locked. I ran in and the room was empty. Out again, on the double. The second door was locked.

A hit man by trade, I can be a bit of a macho guy. But I am not brainless. Countless television shows have cops kicking through doors or driving through with their shoulder. Try it in real life some time. It is not as easy as it looks. A kick is not going to move a good door and, in line with Newton's laws of motion (for every action there is an equal and opposite reaction), if your foot does not go through the door the force of your kick goes right back through your body. You end up on the floor looking foolish most times you try to play the action hero. And as for the shoulder – surgery for a dislocated clavicle is expensive and uncertain.

Brain kicking in at last, I ran back to the girl's room and picked up the lump of masonry I had pulled off her arm. My fingers closed on a wet section and I tried not to think about it. I knew it wasn't water and that was as far as I wanted to know right now. I ran into the corridor and up to the closed door. It took two swings but with the second the wood around the lock splintered. Now it was time for the shoulder.

Here is a thing; if a door opens outward, no amount of shouldering is going to move it in. But this door opened inwards, so once the lock had splintered I was able to barge through. It took only a minute to verify the room was clear. So far, only one casualty on the second floor and she would live.

I moved to the stairs, but here my progress was impeded. It wasn't debris; I could have cleared that. There were no stairs. There was a gaping hole where they once had been. Anyone trapped on the upper floor was going to have to take the window like I had or wait for a fire truck and a ladder.

I bellowed at the top of my voice but heard nothing back. Not a sound. It was mid-afternoon. Perhaps the hostel had been empty? I bellowed again.

"Is no one up there. Is afternoon. All out," came a shout from downstairs. Zloti.

"All?"

"I don't know."

That was helpful. But what could I do? If an angry husband had been chasing me with a machete, I don't think I could have got to what was left of the third floor. Reluctantly I turned. There was only one room left to check and I knew there was no one in there. My own room, the epicentre of the explosion. I knew there was no point in opening the door (metaphorically – as there was no door left) but some ghoulish instinct forced my hand. That, and I wanted to check if was there anything I could salvage. We don't carry travel insurance in my line of business.

Half the wall was missing where the door should have been, so when I edged along the corridor I got a clear view. Most of the wall opposite the door had been blown out, and the tree that had saved my life had taken a bit of a battering. The floor was mostly intact but there was a hole where part had fallen through to the floor beneath. I knew if I stayed near the edge of the floor and avoided the jagged hole I should be safe. So I stepped over the rubble into the room.

Nothing was left. The furniture was in bits, the ceiling ripped out, the portion of the floor that remained covered in rubble.

I could spend a day searching for my possessions and find nothing. But I wasn't inclined to spend a day pulling through the rubble. Because in the middle of the rubble was a leg. And the leg was attached to a bloody and mangled torso. I couldn't see the head but I was fairly sure Humpty Dumpty had nothing on him. There was an unnatural stillness about the body that told me he was very dead. Probably my upstairs neighbour, the Beyoncé fan. Now I would never get the chance to introduce him to real music.

I backed out of the room and returned to the stairs, clambering down to Zloti, who was expertly applying an inflatable splint to the broken arm of the girl I had rescued. I was impressed; the hostel had a well-stocked first aid box.

"It might be safer outside," I suggested.

He shrugged.

"You been in one bombed building, you been in them all. Is good – will not collapse. Supporting wall is strong."

It was my turn to shrug. It is easy to forget that only two decades ago this town had been caught in Armageddon. This afternoon was probably a flashback to Zloti's teenage years and he seemed completely at home. Bombs going off, pretty girls with their limbs hanging loose, all that was missing was the nineties Euro-pop.

"I would feel more comfortable if we brought her out to the side terrace," I insisted.

I took her gently by the other arm and led her out the front of the house and into the side terrace, which was off the street. By now a dozen gawkers had gathered and they stared like ghouls at the pale girl. Blood seeped over the top of the inflatable splint, but you could not see the extent of her injury. I sat her down at a table and one of the onlookers came in, placing a bottle of water in front of us. I smiled my thanks and brought the bottle to the girl's lips.

"Not so bad," said Zloti. "In the war we called this a wanking injury."

That was a new one on me.

"You mean a small injury?"

"No. I mean she will not wank for a few weeks. Unless she has help."

"Or she is right-handed."

"No, the right hand is for turning the pages."

"You are living in the past – all that stuff is on the internet now."

He grinned.

"I know – why you think hostel has wi-fi?"

This was getting surreal. I had to bring him back to reality.

"Who was in the room above mine?"

"Number seven? A German backpacker. Arrived two days ago. He is out."

"No – he is in my room, with his neck broken."

"Shit," said Zloti. "He was a nice guy. And he hadn't paid yet."

Just then we heard the first siren and within seconds I could make out a second. One was a cop car and one was a fire truck. No ambulance yet. I didn't check my watch. I can keep time fairly well in my head and I knew it had been thirteen minutes since the explosion. In a small city that was a very slow response time. And the girl with the wanking injury would have to wait a bit longer for help unless a third siren began sounding fairly quickly. I turned to Zloti.

"You look after her and I'll go out to the street and show them where to come," I offered. I stood and walked from the terrace to the growing crowd outside.

"Is she going to be all right?" asked the guy who had donated the bottle. I nodded. I gently pushed my way to the back of the crowd, as if I was going to the street to greet the emergency services. But as I got to the edge of the crowd I planned to slip across the street and down a narrow lane between two buildings. I turned from the crowd and stepped away.

I felt a strong hand grasp my shoulder and turned sharply. A big cop had a firm grip on me. As I squirmed slightly I felt his fingers tighten. I looked into his dark eyes and saw nothing but grim determination.

FOUR

It took a moment for my heart to stop racing and I immediately began running scenarios through my head. Had he seen me coming from the building? Was I covered in debris? Did someone tip him off? The most important question was how was I going to escape from him and get away before the rest of the cavalry arrived?

I was spared having to make a decision.

"Da li postoje mnoge povreden?"

I looked at him blankly and made the universal gesture of incomprehension, shrugging my shoulders and shaking my head.

"Jebeno stranac," he muttered as he let me go and turned to someone else in the crowd. I didn't need a dictionary to know he had called me a fucking foreigner, but I took no offence. I quickly stepped across the road and into the alley. As I reached the end of the lane I glanced back and saw the crowd part as more cops began pulling up. I turned my head and kept walking. This was no time to play the hero.

The first rule of staying alive is to avoid being seen. People who read too many spy books assume guys like me spend our time glancing in shop windows to detect reflected spooks. Not true. The pros don't waste their time walking behind you, skulking in doorways every time you turn around. A good pro will use the landscape. And in a city that means CCTV cameras. They are all over the place. They were what I had to avoid.

I walked down the side of the street at a normal walking pace, but with my head down. The cameras are always high up and keeping your head down nullifies facial recognition software. The alley led to a business street and these are the ones with the cameras. Residential areas are safe. So I turned from the city centre and began walking out of town. Soon I was on streets with fewer shops, more apartment blocks. Still dangerous but getting better. After twenty minutes I was on what looked like safe ground. Rows of small houses, kids playing on the road, occasional corner shops.

There was a small park with a playground. I entered it but walked well away from the swings. A man on his own near a playground always draws the wrong sort of attention. So I found a shady tree and sat beneath it. There was no one around and I could see most of my surroundings. And if someone tried to approach me from the rear I would hear the snapping of twigs. Of course, I was still vulnerable to sniper shots, but I was not that paranoid. Not yet.

I took out the cell phone and keyed in a number I knew from memory. There was the inevitable wait as the local network hooked up with the satellite, which bounced back to the network in the States. Longer, because I was using a specially encrypted satellite phone that looked like a regular smartphone. I counted off twenty-eight seconds in my head before the ring tone told me the call had been put through.

Four rings, then he picked up.

"Hi man," he drawled.

Bill loves a pun. Especially one he considers a bit inappropriate. He thought this was a hilarious way to open a phone conversation. I disagreed. I think anyone who sees a pun there needs to do a lot of growing up. And I wasn't feeling the hilarity today. Not by a long stretch.

"What the hell is happening?"

"And a good day to you too, Eli," he replied.

I sighed. It was going to be one of those conversations. I could picture him in his office in Langley, looking out over rolling hills and trees, the small figurine of Homer Simpson grinning back at him from the window ledge. He could be an ass at times but, like all good friends, he had my back.

"Bill, I'm stuck over here and it has all gone to hell," I said, not wasting breath on the formalities.

"Stuck where?"

That stumped me. Surely he knew?

"In Bosnia, you moron."

"What are you doing in that godforsaken hole?"

"Working for you."

"Are you sure?"

"Sorry, my mistake. I'm here to collect orchids for the British Museum. Of course I'm sure. You put out a hit on Jarko Radoslav."

"He's small fry. Why would we put a hit out on him?"

"Ours not to reason why. Ours just to do or die. Or do *and* die in my case."

"Start from the beginning," he suggested.

So I did. I told him how I had responded to the ad on the Magic Bistro. That's when things started to get weird.

"We haven't posted there in a while," he said.

Around me in the park I could hear the birds twittering in the trees, the distant sound of kids shouting, the most distant drone of traffic. My head felt fuzzy. None of this was right. I should be relaxing in my room, spending one last evening in Mostar, one good dinner and a bottle of wine and a flight home in the morning. I could feel a vein throbbing in my head.

"You in a secure location?"

I looked around the park. One of the kids had a clear bead on me if he used a slingshot. There was a bird overhead that could crap on me. No baddies.

"Secure enough."

"Take the battery out of your phone for an hour. I will be in touch then."

Straightforward security provisions and I had already forgotten them. Phones can be tracked. But not when the battery is disconnected. I hung up and disabled the phone. I had an hour to kill. I couldn't kill it in the park in case someone was tracking.

Nonchalantly, hands in my pockets, I strolled the suburbs, nodding at old men on street corners and watching an impromptu soccer game on a bit of waste ground. Outside, I was a man killing time. Inside, I was not myself. Pretty girls passed and I didn't look. That is always a sign the mind is not focused.

I didn't last the hour. Fifty-five minutes in, on a long wide street with low apartment blocks, I slipped the battery into the phone and powered it up. Almost instantly it pinged: incoming message.

My heart beating, I opened the message without even checking who the sender was. It was a simple one word message: "Well?"

My brother, still on about the porn video.

With a surge of irritation I jabbed out a rapid response: "She told me it is lesbian porn, so nothing to worry about." I hit send. That would put his knickers in a twist for a bit.

FIVE

Seven minutes later the call I was waiting for came in. Bill, back in Langley.

"Bad news," he began. No preamble. "Like I thought, we didn't put that job up. I've had the tech guys run it through the system. Someone hacked us, used our identity to put up the post."

"Shit."

"It gets worse. It was a sophisticated hack. You were the only one who could see the post. So they wanted you, and only you, to take the hit."

I let that sink in for a minute. It made no sense.

"You still there?"

"Why would someone pick on me like this? I don't see the point."

"We're still working on the whos and the whys," said Bill. I could hear sounds behind him. He wasn't calling from a secure location. But he was in the heart of CIA headquarters in Virginia so I suppose every corner of the building was secure. He didn't have to scan the street for strange men as he spoke.

"Give me a minute, Eli."

There were indistinct murmurings, Bill's voice occasionally rising above the background. Finally, he was back on the line.

"Wow," he began.

"That helps," I replied.

"We know who hacked us. Or at least, who is behind it."

He paused for a few heartbeats and I waited. I could hear the distress in his voice when he resumed.

"It's a big fish. Amel Dugalic."

Now I got the hesitation. No one had heard of Dugalic. His name had not hit the papers or risen in public consciousness. There was a reason; he was the hidden power broker who had been one of the beneficiaries of the war in the early nineties. He had pulled the strings behind the scenes, and made millions. He was a money man for one of the warlords on the Bosnian side who had also played a double game by working for a Serbian faction at the same time. Playing both sides, he couldn't lose. In the new Bosnia he kept a low profile, but at least four factions owed him allegiance. I knew none of this; Bill had to fill me in. His account left me confused.

"What has that to do with me?"

"Don't you see? Radoslav was a small fry. He was never on our list. But we are building a case against Dugalic. Bring him down and you bring down four gangs with him, one with ties to fundamentalist Islam. He's our target and you're the man we're hoping to send in. We're going to drop a hundred big ones on this guy and you'll pull the trigger."

"Unless I'm dead."

"Exactly. Dugalic must have found out. So he hacked our account. Now you're in Bosnia and you have killed one of his business rivals. A win for him. And he kills you. Double win for him."

"So I have to kill him now?"

"You have to get out of Bosnia now. He's too well protected. You'll be back."

"I'm not the terminator."

"Exactly – and even Arnie could be killed. You've got to run, boy. Run."

I sighed. So much for my relaxing dinner, glass of wine and easy trip home.

"Can you ...?"

"No," he said, before I could complete my question. He was right; I knew the rules. I don't work for American intelligence. I am a bounty hunter, a freelance. If something goes wrong I am on my own. It is the only way this game can work. It provides complete deniability for the governments that use my unique services.

"Do your best to get out on your own, and I'll see if can I put together a plan B, but it will be strictly off the books if it is possible. Don't wait for it because it might not happen. You're on your own. I'll pray for you, buddy."

That bad.

I spent the night back in the park. Mostar in summer is not so bad for al fresco sleeping and there was no concierge to make note of my passport and alert watchers to my presence. I had very little with me, just a few essentials. The phone, of course. That was never more than an arm's length away. And my wallet. That had been hidden close to the assassination site for the four days I had staked out Radoslav and had been in my pocket ever since. It contained a number of junk credit cards and one library card that was my real credit card. It looked just like a library card but had the full chip and pin and magnetic strip and worked perfectly throughout Europe. Because of its disguise it would not reveal my real identity. I also had my passport – well, one of them. The Mark Wilson one. I also had around sixty Bosnian convertible marka and a few coins. That amounted to less than thirty euro. Damn all use to me.

It got chilly after midnight but I found a low wall and curled down in its lea, taking some shelter from the light summer breeze. I had nothing to double as a pillow and I can't say it was a comfortable night. But in the morning I was up bright and early. By seven I was walking the empty streets and at eight I found a café for breakfast. After, I hit the bathroom. I looked like hell. My eyes were red, I had stubble and it looked as if I had been sleeping rough. I tidied myself up as best as I could and killed another two hours before taking the bus for the short ride to Ortijes and the airport.

Mostar has the second busiest airport in Bosnia, due to its nearness to Medugorje, a major Catholic pilgrimage centre. But it would be exaggerating to call it a thriving aviation centre. It was a small low building in the middle of nowhere, with a sleepy feel to it. Security would be lax, with just a few pilgrims and locals heading to Sarajevo. I was tense, but getting through should be no problem.

Nonetheless, I took precautions. The first thing I had to determine was whether my passport was hot; would it set alarm bells ringing? I entered the terminal building, and quickly got my bearings. Only a few airlines used the facility and I could see from the departure board that I had two hours to my flight, the Blue Panorama charter to Rome. There were about sixty people in the concourse and it was not difficult to spot someone on the same flight as me. He was a businessman in his forties travelling with a younger woman. She might have been his wife. She might have been his secretary, or mistress, or both. He had his travel documents in his hand when I bumped into him.

"I am so sorry," I muttered. Then I said it in Bosnian, and Italian. Covering all the bases. I smiled weakly and then bent to pick up his passport for him. That was when the switch happened. I did it deftly and he never suspected a thing. I put his ticket into his hand, too, and smiled again.

"Nessun problemo," he said. Italian. Going home.

As his wife/secretary/mistress fussed around him, I went into the toilet, emerging a few minutes later with sunglasses I had stolen from the backpack of a traveller. I stayed on the edges of the crowd until the flight was called then got into a position where I could see the Italian businessman, but not be in his line of sight. What would happen next was simple. His passport would be rejected because it was not his passport. It was Mark Wilson's. If that was all that happened I would make my way up to him, apologise once more and put the situation right. But it might not be that simple. The next few minutes would tell.

The line moved, edging towards the bored looking officials at the security check. Mark Wilson was at least ten people in front of me. I could reach him quickly or I could fade into the background, depending on how things went. The butterflies were circling my innards. I was constantly scanning the crowd, alert for any dangers. That was when I saw her. The tall woman I had passed shortly after the assassination, the woman with no daddy issues. With my shades on and the dust washed from my hair she probably couldn't recognise me but I instinctively tried to avoid eye contact. Using my peripheral vision I could see her looking at me a moment too long, but she was probably trying to place a face in a crowd, nothing more. Tourists bump into each other constantly in foreign countries and I had nothing to worry about on that score. My worry was now near the top of the line.

The Italian reached the passport official. I watched as he pushed the passport forward and got ready to walk through to the gate. The official looked at the passport and was about to hand it back when he paused. He looked up at the businessman then back down at the passport. The pictures weren't an exact match but passport pictures all look like convict mugshots. Now he would discover that the name did not match the name on the ticket, which was what I was interested in.

I couldn't hear what was being said above the sound of the other travellers but it was obvious that some discussion was taking place. The official handed the passport to a colleague, who looked at it, then at the Italian businessman. Heads dropped and a discussion followed in rapid Bosnian. Both men looked up and the first nodded slightly. Immediately two large policemen appeared from nowhere, taking positions on either side of the businessman. They took him by the elbows and began leading him to a door at the side of the concourse. Now I could hear what he was saying because he had raised his voice and the line had gone silent. He was speaking in English, trying to explain to the two policemen that he had bumped into a fellow passenger and that was not his passport. But they kept him moving, and a moment later he disappeared.

I felt a pang of guilt. Obviously the name Mark Wilson on the passport had triggered a security alert and the Italian faced a few hours of frustrating delay and interrogation. My question was answered; if I had tried to board with that passport I would have been hauled away. Whoever had set me up had been very thorough. But I had been more thorough. All I had to do was walk up with the Italian passport, explain about the collision, take his ticket from the security desk and leave the Mark Wilson one there, and board. Simple. The sense of relief that I was on the way again banished all guilt, and I sighed.

I flipped open the stolen passport to see how closely I resembled the man I was meant to be and to check my new name. That was when I knew I was in trouble.

I had his mistress's passport!

SIX

Some situations cannot be made right. I would not be flying today. I made my way out of the airport and used some of my precious supplies of Bosnian convertible marka to get a taxi back to town. I didn't want to hang around waiting for the bus in case the cops figured out the Italian was innocent quicker than cops normally figure such things out. I jumped in the first cab and gave the only address I knew in the city; the bombed hostel.

Luckily enough I had the sense to stop a few blocks early and get out. The hostel could be under surveillance. I walked away, towards the more commercial centre. Soon I saw what I was looking for. One more test to see how screwed I was. I took my card out of my wallet and put it in the hole in the wall, keying in my PIN. A notice came up in the Cyrillic alphabet. It could have been a message asking me what service I required. But the flashing yellow triangle with the exclamation mark in it made that unlikely. I hit the button that I know means to cancel, but the machine kept flashing and my card was not returned to me.

Now I knew. I was screwed.

I had been set up by an expert. Despite being confident he would kill me in the hostel explosion, he had covered all bases by flagging my passport and by hacking enough systems to get my card rejected. I had no documents, no money and no way home.

That's what friends are for. I rang Bill.

"You're right. You're screwed," he assured me when I had brought him up to speed. "And you know I can't help. What you need is a friend. Are there any other guys in the business in the area?"

On the face of it, not a bad suggestion. We are a small elite group, us big bounty hunters. But we are hardly friends. Friendly rivals in some cases, bitter rivals in other cases. There were a few among the Brits that I could count on, a smaller number of Americans, and very few of the Europeans. And what were the odds of any of them being in the same part of Europe?

"Give me an hour," said Bill.

He didn't need the hour. Thirty-five minutes later my phone beeped and I picked up at the first ring.

"I have good news and I have bad news. I will give you both together. The only possible friend you have is in Dubrovnik, but it is La Donna."

The silence on the phone stretched. Telling me that La Donna was my lifeline was like telling a man in a dark cave that he could light the fuse on a stick of dynamite and it would provide him with illumination. True, but most of us would choose to curse the darkness. La Donna and I had a history and it is never good to have a history with a woman like her. I had left my religion behind me in my teens, but I still felt the urge to cross myself.

"Are you still there?" Bill asked eventually.

"Where is she based?" I replied. I would embrace the madness and light the fuse.

Getting to Dubrovnik would be the problem. I had to organise it with no money and no papers. The papers weren't a major issue. I felt the Italian's passport would get me through border patrol into Croatia easily enough. It is slack on the road. Most cars are waved through without even lowering a window. But I didn't have a car, and 140 km was too far to walk.

The obvious solution was to steal a car. It would not be difficult with my skill set. And if you pick the right car it won't be reported missing until long after you have abandoned it. It is a risk, but normally a safe one. What bothered me was that Dugalic, or whoever he had hired to do his dirty work, was a step ahead of me all the time. So the risk was too great.

My brother, the most conservative and conventional man I know, loved to trot out business jargon like Think Outside the Box. Easy to sneer, but he might be right. I remembered an old bar story. It might work. It would be risky, but a life without risks would make me my brother.

Walking casually but observing my surroundings like a pro, I made my way back to the bombed hostel. I was surprised to see a portacabin in the small courtyard and much of the rubble already cleared. Back in the UK that would have been a crime scene and it might have taken months before the rebuild began. I was impressed.

Zloti was running around like a general ordering the troops. Construction workers were moving about in dusty overalls.

There was a bustle and energy to the scene. He saw me and grinned.

"Mr Mark Wilson – are you here for your luggage?" And he laughed.

I laughed too, despite not being very happy about losing everything.

"Keep it another week," I joked. "I need your help with my next trip."

"You stay Bosnia or you go to another country?"

"I have to visit a friend in Dubrovnik, and it is his birthday. I am going to surprise him with a cake."

"Cake is good surprise. Cake with girl inside, surprise is better."

"The cake is enough. And a clown. He is on holiday with his family and I want to bring a clown to entertain the family."

He looked surprised. I elaborated.

"In England it is normal to have a clown at a party."

"Here is for circus only."

But on my insistence he borrowed a phone directory from a neighbour and went to the business pages. His face showed his surprise.

"Is six children's entertainer clowns in Mostar," he said. "You use my phone, you call one."

That was a great idea, considering my command of Bosnian did not extend beyond Hello and Goodbye. Instead, I pointed at him.

"You make the call for me."

Ten minutes later the deal was done. The first two clowns

had turned down the gig, but the third said yes. For two hundred euros he would drive down to Dubrovnik, surprise the British family and do his show, then make balloon animals for all the kids. For another twenty he agreed to let me ride with him. He would pick me up in thirty minutes.

There was one last part to my plan. Using my remaining few notes, I went to a bakery and bought a simple cake, but had it placed in a very elaborate box, tied with a fancy ribbon. I was ready to escape from Mostar.

True to his word, the clown arrived in his beat-up little estate car shortly after I got back with the cake. We shook hands. I was a bit surprised at his appearance. I don't know what I was expecting, but not someone who looked like a miserable hill farmer with a battered suitcase and two plastic carrier bags. I don't think he would have passed the Magic Circle entrance exam. But he passed my test. He was the perfect cover for my escape. We drove through the outskirts of Mostar and joined the M6. It was a good highway but the surface was rough and our nail bucket rattled as we drove. When we merged with the M17 it got a bit worse, if that was possible. The journey would take a little less than two hours, and though the kilometres passed quickly the time did not. At the start, we tried to pass a few remarks but his English was as bad as my Bosnian, which would not bode well for any British kids he might end up entertaining at our destination.

An hour and forty minutes into the journey the traffic began to slow imperceptibly. A few clicks later there was a small tailback and a single portacabin at the side of the road. A soldier was standing there, with a few others inside the cabin. He looked hot and tired and not too interested in the passing traffic. Cars slowed down, he nodded them on. More cars took their place, he nodded them on. We were edging closer. Would he nod us on? I had my Italian passport ready.

As we reached the top of the queue, my clown reached across me and flipped open the glove compartment. He took out a red clown nose and popped it on his face. He looked out at the soldier, whose face lit up. He stuck his head in the window and the two men jabbered at each other for a few minutes, then the soldier dropped his rifle and took out a cell phone. He took a selfie with the red-nosed driver, then waved us on, a huge grin on his face.

The driver put the nose back in the glove compartment then said in broken English: "I did his party ten years ago."

"Small world," I replied. The driver looked at me blankly.

Almost immediately after crossing the border the road surface improved dramatically. I could smell the sea on the light summer breeze and ten minutes later I could see it glinting in the distance to our right. The countryside was slightly less arid than the interior as we approached the coast. Even the cars seemed a bit newer, but I suspect that was my imagination. I liked Croatia. It was not Bosnia.

Within twenty minutes we were in the heart of Dubrovnik. Now for the tricky bit. It was not dangerous, but I had to struggle to keep a straight face. When I had hired the clown I had to give him an address, so I had gone on the web and found a room through AirBnB. That was the address I had

given him. I was curious to see where I had picked out. I had
to admit I was impressed. The room was in a modern house
on a quiet street. The street was on a hill in the newer section
of the town, overlooking the walled old quarter and the small
old harbour in the distance. It looked like a bit of a walk
into town, but if I had been a real tourist I would have been
delighted.

Now was the moment.

I turned to the clown and tried to explain as best I could.
With a mixture of wild gestures, smiles and the pigeon English
we always use with those who don't speak the language I
did my best to make him understand that I was going to go
into the house and get them ready for him to make his grand
entrance. I pointed to the cake and told him to bring it in with
him. He grinned.

"Five minutes. I put on costume, get show to the ready."

I gave him a thumbs up, he gave me a thumbs up, and I got
out of the car. Still smiling I walked to the house and walked
around the side towards the back. I turned and smiled. He
smiled back. I walked on, turned the corner of the house
and found myself on the rear balcony, where the view was
outstanding. I think it was outstanding. To be honest, I didn't
look. Because when I came around the corner on to the
balcony I disturbed two women sunbathing topless in what
they thought was privacy. I smiled pleasantly at them – I was
doing a lot of smiling that afternoon – then walked past and
vaulted over the low railing to the neighbouring balcony. From
there steps led to a lane. I didn't know where it would lead but

I walked briskly down it. I wanted to be as far away as possible from the balcony when the clown walked into the topless beauties.

I no longer had to keep a straight face and I was grinning widely. I felt bad for the clown but it had only cost him a few hours and some petrol money. And he got a cake out of it.

Now I just had to find out where the hell I was, make my way to the harbour and locate La Donna. And we had a history. That wiped the smile off my face.

SEVEN

I killed another few hours, which wasn't difficult. Dubrovnik is a lot more modern and cosmopolitan than Mostar. Another thing that made it easy was that I spent much of the time cursing my brother. He had sent another text. It read: "WTF! Why didn't she tell me she came out? Can you stop her?"

He is so strait-laced he never swears in real life. For him to even think of writing WTF showed just how upset he was that his precious air of respectability was under threat from the black sheep of the family. Funny how the dancer, bringing joy to thousands, is the black sheep, while the hired assassin is not. But then none of my family actually know what I do for a living. They think I lead extreme adventure tours in odd parts of the world. I do, but it is a tour of one and the only extreme adventure is big game hunting. Only two people are involved in each adventure, and normally only one returns.

I ignored the text. Jane is the nicest woman you could meet and if she is a lesbian it will come as a surprise to me and her boyfriend.

Dubrovnik began as a small walled city, heavily fortified. From the hills around you could look down and see a modern sprawl, but at the centre there was an area bounded on three sides by the thick walls of the medieval fortification and on the fourth side by the sea. The houses in this section all had the distinctive red tiled roofs of that ancient era and the streets were very narrow. The rest of the town had wider streets and more modern roofs. It was as if someone had taken an aerial shot of the city and put a reddish orange stamp near the centre of the sea edge, I thought when I first looked down. It was a town of ups and downs and you would want your wind to explore it properly. I did some exploring and some coffee drinking to kill the time. I found a bookshop and spent two hours trying to bludgeon my way through *Ulysses* again. The first few chapters were a joy, and after that ... God, that man needed an editor.

I waited until nearly nine before I made my way to the small hotel on the edge of the harbour where La Donna was staying. My unerring instinct in these matters, and a text from Bill, led me right to her lair. What can I say about her? The first thing is that La Donna is not her name. I have no idea what her real name is, just as she has no idea what mine is. That is the way in the shadowy underworld. We go by nicknames, signatures of convenience and false papers. She called herself La Donna because she thought it meant lady in Italian. I called myself Eli, after one of the three actors in the spaghetti western *The Good, The Bad and the Ugly*. That trilogy of westerns captures the spirit of the bounty hunter, and people in the business accepted my nickname. Few of them knew that it is also my real name.

La Donna's choice of nickname told me she was far less Italian than she claimed. Even my schoolboy grasp of the language was enough to know that La Donna means woman while lady translates as La Signora. I guessed she was from the former Yugoslavia, probably special forces or secret police before the break-up of the country.

Instead of joining one of the warring factions she had gone to Italy and hooked up with the Camorra, or Neapolitan mafia. Her job was roughly similar to mine. She carried out contract killings for the bounty. But after that we differed. I have my rules. She has none if legend is to be believed. I knew she had killed many times more than I. Men, women and children – it made no difference. And collateral damage was just part of the fun. She was a cold-hearted bitch who was looking at psychopathic in the rear-view mirror. If you can judge a man by his friends I was screwed.

As I approached the hotel I could see it was just the sort of place she would gravitate towards. The seedy run-down structure was obviously not a tourist trap. I knew the bar would be full and that the young women propping up the counter would be available for rent by the hour, or for shorter periods if that was more your thing. Not a classy establishment and everyone drinking would be local. Everyone staying would be either a sailor or a travelling sales rep.

I went in and pushed past a leggy blonde to the bar, calling for a beer. A couple of people looked at me, but no one cared. The blonde did try with a come-hither smile, but she gave up quickly when she realised I wasn't buying it, or her. Leaning my back against the bar as I sipped the cold beer, I scanned the room. It was easy to spot her. She could have passed for a double of the late Princess Diana. She had the same tall body, the same short bobbed blonde hair, the same haughty regal air. But there were some subtle differences. One was that she was stacked like Di never was. It may have been a push-up bra, or it may have been the amount she spent on surgery. I knew she had had surgery. As I said, we had history.

Another difference was that she had an attitude that Diana never had. Raw sensuality oozed from every pore. She was dressed in a black jacket with a scarlet blouse beneath it, the buttons straining to breaking point. She was sitting right under a no smoking sign with a cigarette between her fingers. The four guys around her all looked ready with a light.

Then she saw me.

I could see the startled look register on her face. It was gone a microsecond later and she was looking right through me. A pro to the end. I might be on a job. She wasn't going to blow my cover. I smiled slightly to tell her it was all right, then looked through her. No one watching could have seen the glance we exchanged. After all, she might be working and I might blow her cover. But no, she nodded, and I knew we were safe. As I walked towards her table she stood, towering over the four men. She towered over me too, in heels that made her look like a goddess and that were incredibly effective as a stabbing implement. Just ask José Antifermo, whose heart had been pierced during a sexual encounter with a tall woman who was never identified. I don't know what crime merited José's name appearing on a mafia hit list, but I hope he died happy. Knowing La Donna as I do I am sure he died at the peak of his happiness. That would have appealed to her kinky side.

"Darling," she gushed, as she stepped forward and threw her arms around me. I leaned in to kiss her on the cheek, but she turned her head and caught me full on the lips. It was a good kiss – I counted four Mississippis before she removed her tongue from my mouth.

"Scoot," she said to one of her four acolytes. He obligingly stood up and I took the seat beside her. He didn't look happy, but perhaps he got something out of being bossed around by an Amazon. She turned to the other three.

"It's been real nice. Maybe we can do it again sometime."

The party was over. The guys knew it. Reluctantly they stood. The first guy tried to say something but his voice faltered out as she fixed her pale blue eyes on him. The second and third shuffled away. But the fourth – he wasn't so easy to shift.

He fixed me with a glare that would have frozen hot soup and said: "I was buying the lady a drink."

"And now I am," I said, trying to keep my voice level and calm. I even tried a smile but it was no good.

"You are not welcome here," he went on.

"Oh darling," interrupted La Donna, "you can buy me a drink later. Now I simply must catch up with my old friend Eli."

"No. He will come back later. Now you are with me."

This was getting silly. I stood up to leave.

"Sit down." She turned to the other man. "Don't be ridiculous."

"I am not being ridiculous. This man will now leave."

He was speaking with exaggerated slowness, like a drunk trying to appear sober. That made him dangerous. He was not drunk enough to be out of control but he was certainly drunk enough to have lost his inhibitions. A fight was on the cards and the last thing a man on the run needs is a fight. You don't want to draw attention to yourself. I stood and began to walk away.

"That's it, go," he taunted. "Little sissy boy."

I'm a big boy. I can take it. I kept walking until I reached the bar. I nodded at the man behind the counter and pointed towards a tap. He smiled and took down a glass, filling it with lager. All good. He pushed the glass towards me, but our friend had left La Donna and come up to the bar.

"I thought you were leaving," he said. He picked up the glass and I knew what was coming next. I might have taken it if I had a change of clothes. But I didn't, so I gripped his wrist with more power than he expected and squeezed. His grip on the glass began to waver and with my other hand I took it and replaced it on the counter. I was not going to get the contents poured over me tonight. I looked at him and smiled ruefully.

"You could have walked away," I said. "But if you insist on dancing, I will dance. Out the back door and we'll do it."

I let go his arm and nodded towards the rear door, which I assumed led to a yard at the back of the premises. After feeling the power of my grip he had sobered slightly, but he couldn't back down. So he walked ahead of me to the door. At the last minute I drew level with him and pushed open the door.

"After you."

He walked out the door into the small yard and I quickly stepped back inside, drawing the door closed. There was a small bolt that I pulled across, locking him out. I heard a bellow of fury from outside and the door shook as he pounded it with his fists. But I could ignore that. The guys in the bar following the action laughed. That would infuriate him more if he could hear it, but I didn't think he could. The door was not that flimsy. I returned to the bar. He would fume for a few minutes then slink away. Problem solved.

I picked up my glass and stepped across to La Donna's table, sitting down and shrugging. She had a sardonic smile on her face. She was loving this. I took a sip and put the glass down. I was in no rush. I needed to ask this unstable woman for help, and it would not be an easy thing to ask. She needed to be played.

Just then the front door of the tavern banged open and I didn't need to turn to know that my friend was back.

EIGHT

The drunk should have swallowed his humiliation and gone home, but obviously he believed he could take me and there he was, silhouetted against the entrance. I had time to half turn as I heard a glass bottle break. As I completed the turn I took in the situation at a glance. He had smashed a wine bottle and was charging forward, the ragged end of the bottle coming at me like a vicious jaw. I half stood to meet his attack but kept my head down, ducking slightly as he moved in for the strike.

His first blow sailed harmlessly over my left shoulder and left him over-extended. His momentum carried him forward and I continued to rise, turning into him. My shoulder caught him under the arm and I tackled him hard. He stumbled forward and only luck prevented him from hitting the floor. He managed to get one hand on a table, then straightened and came at me again. This time I stood and faced him. He drew his arm back, a mistake. Never telegraph your move. Then he swung viciously at my face. It was what I expected. An amateur, and drunk with it. No other move would do but the obvious. All I had to do was drop my knees and roll my head. The wild roundhouse sailed harmlessly over my head and I stepped into him again, this time clenching my fist and driving a left hook viciously under his ribs. I could feel him deflate as the air left his lungs in a rush. I straightened and hit him under the jaw with my right.

The mistake amateurs make is to hit someone on the head with a fist. The human skill is a heavy lump of bone, hard as stone. If you hit it full force you will probably break your knuckles and do very little damage to your opponent. I did not make that mistake. I drew my fingers back and hit him with the heel of my hand. I could feel the satisfying crack as I made contact. With luck, his jaw was not broken, but he was out cold as soon as I hit him. I managed to grab the front of his shirt as he fell and guided him to the ground. I didn't want his head to bounce off the hard floor and cause more damage. The last thing I needed was cops crawling all over the place.

I checked his breathing. Heavy and laboured. No real damage done. He would wake in a few minutes and nurse the mother and father of a headache tomorrow. But I wouldn't be up for assault. As I was leaning over him I could see his wallet jutting out of his back pocket. I am no thief but am not adverse to taking a loan when offered. I slipped the wallet into my own pocket.

I looked at the barman, but he turned away. Not his business. That was good.

Just then one of La Donna's original fan club came forward. He tapped me gently on the shoulder.

"I take him home now. He sleep it off."

"Thanks," I said.

We smiled knowingly at each other. The fight was over. There would be no repercussions.

I sat down and faced La Donna. She smiled, licking her lower lip seductively.

"My big man," she said. "You handled him like a pro."

Hardly a compliment, considering that I am a pro. That is what I do, handle difficult men. And I have known La Donna long enough not to fall for her superficial charms. But then she ran one fingernail delicately down my arm, her nail barely moving the little hairs. And I felt it, a shiver run right through to my core. The woman had electricity.

"In town on a job?" she purred.

"Don't you know it. Done and dusted and now I am on my way home."

"The Radoslav hit. I heard."

"I'm saying nothing. Walls have ears."

Damn, but she was well informed. She must have spotted the post on the Magic Café. Then it hit me – there was no post on the Café. That was a hack, only seen by me. A shadow of suspicion crossed my mind, but she went on: "I heard he had been taken out by a real professional. You are in the region. I put two and two together. What did you get for it?"

"Not enough for a Ferrari, but enough to buy you a wonderful bottle of bubbly."

"A mind-reader and a killer. The perfect gentleman."

She looked up and nodded knowingly at the bartender who reached down into the cool cabinet behind him. . The good stuff was coming out. I hoped my newly-acquired wallet could take the hit.

It was good champagne. The bubbles tickled the roof of my mouth delightfully as they danced down my throat. I could feel the quick rush to my head, which settled just as quickly.

You could drink this all night. And you could end up dead as a result, I reminded myself.

"So," she said, looking deeply into my eyes. "You kill the man and then you seek out La Donna."

I shook my head vigorously.

"I just came in here to while away the evening and was as surprised as you when I saw who was in the bar."

"Nonsense. You are not a drinker. A man like you would go to a play to kill the evening, or to a whorehouse. So trouble brings you here. Did someone make you?"

"I should be insulted. Of course no one made me. I got clean away."

"And yet you are here."

I sighed. She wasn't going to buy my innocent routine. I wasn't surprised. She is as sharp as they come.

"There were complications," I admitted. "And now I need a gun. And a few thousand to get me home. Mainly the money."

She looked at me, her eyes boring straight through. She let the silence stretch, an old interrogation technique. I broke first.

"And some documents."

She nodded.

"Now we come to it. You are in deep shit. And I knew that before you came into the bar, so don't try to bullshit me. You carried out a hit on a warlord and the warlord that ordered the hit doesn't want you going home to spend his money. You see, I am well informed. I also know that word has gone around that no one is to help you."

This was news to me. My situation was worse than I thought.

"We have history," I reminded her. Both good and bad history I thought, but hoped she would only remember the good.

"For old times' sake I would like to help you, but I won't," she said. "There are two reasons I won't help you. The first is that my employers have asked me, as a courtesy, not to get involved. And the second is that I am very busy at the moment."

I looked at her and she smiled.

"Oh yes, I am very busy tonight. Even as we speak I am fucking a man. Sorry, that is a bit crude, but what I am doing to that man you could not call making love. And coitus sounds so clinical."

This time I let the silence grow, not in an effort to get her to reveal more, but because I was completely lost. Perhaps she had drunk more than I thought.

"I see that you do not believe me," she said, standing. "Come, I will show you."

NINE

I followed her up the stairs at the back of the bar, to an upper floor where a few dingy rooms were rented. Knowing the type of area, I bet you could have got one by the night or by the hour. The first two rooms had doors ajar so were still available. The final room on the corridor was closed. This was the door she approached. She took a key from her pocket and inserted it in the lock.

"You will love this," she said. I had my doubts.

She opened the door and my doubts were confirmed. It was a small room with a dusty brown carpet that hadn't seen shampoo in my lifetime. The bed was half-way between single and queen size, with an off-white throw over it that had also seen better days and better decades. The walls were painted orange and a horrid photo of a harbour scene swung crookedly over the head of the bed. A single light bulb, no shade, hung in the middle of the room, and the window was closed, giving it an unnatural feeling of stuffiness and heat.

However bad the room was it paled into insignificance beside what was on the bed. Stretched on the dirty white throw was a thin young man with dark hair, completely naked except for his nylon striped necktie. He was spread-eagled, his wrists handcuffed to the head of the bed and his ankles tied with rope to the end of the bed. He looked terrified and his head spun towards us as the door opened.

"Please..." he pleaded.

"This is my lover for tonight," said La Donna, walking forward and stroking his cheek gently. "Aren't you, my dear? Such a sweet young man. I feel it will be an exceptionally pleasurable encounter."

He flinched from her touch, but she didn't seem to notice. She had a strange light in her eyes that chilled me like a shadow passing over my soul. It wasn't madness. She was in too much control for that. And it wasn't evil. But it wasn't far off either.

She ran her finger down his cheek and along his neck, passing gently to his chest. Slowly, smiling into his frightened face, she ran her finger down his thin hairless chest, down past his navel, slowing when she reached his waist. As she reached his pubic hair her smile broadened.

"Such a sweet young man," she purred, grasping his flaccid penis gently. As her fingers closed about his member she began to stroke it gently as he squirmed.

"Please..." he whispered.

"Hush my sweet," she said, continuing to caress him. Her other hand was delicately brushing his chest and she held his eyes with a smile. As he squirmed, unable to move properly because of the constraints, she continued with her soft kneading motion, and slowly his penis began to grow until it was semi erect. He was fighting it but, as all men under fifty know (and over fifty remember with regret), the little man has a mind of his own. His body was betraying his earnest desire not to get aroused. She was good.

I was very uncomfortable. This was an intimate moment and

I had no business watching it. It also felt uncommonly like
a rape. I wanted to be anywhere outside of that room. But I
needed her help. I forced my face not to register the disgust I
felt.

Then she took him in her mouth, and I had to look away.
It was only a few minutes. I don't believe she finished him
off. She brought him to a peak, then straightened up. Perhaps
keeping him on the brink was part of her game. She leaned
forward, her breasts crushing against his chest, and clasped
him by the cheeks, bringing her lips down hard against his. The
savage kiss lasted as long as the kiss she greeted me with, then
she was standing and grinning at me.

"We will have so much fun tonight," she said. "So you can
see, I am too busy to help you, even if my employers would let
me. But I do have time to let you buy me another drink before
I come back to my lover boy."

She smiled at him, then took the tie from around his neck
and swiftly tied it around his mouth, gagging him. He was able
to breathe and able to grunt. But he wouldn't be able to cry
for help. I followed her out to the corridor and she closed and
locked the door behind her.

We went back down to the bar and had another glass of the
bubbly. My face betrayed nothing. Actually, I managed to grin
like a schoolboy in on a prank.

"I didn't know you were into games," I said.

"All sex is a game," she replied. "Normally the men make the
rules, but today I have turned that around. In this game I am

the dungeon master, he is the slave."

"Does he get to enjoy the game?"

"Of course. All men are animals and at the end I will give him his moment of release. That is all a man wants. For a woman, it is all foreplay."

"And what you were doing upstairs was foreplay?"

"But of course. And he loved it."

"He didn't seem to be loving it."

"You can't read the signs. His mind was still full of thoughts. Those thoughts and worries will go and he will lose himself in the experience."

I shrugged. I don't get S&M play. My tastes are very vanilla. The lifestyle I have chosen is not conducive of lasting relationships, but I don't live like a monk. I take my chances when I can get them, and I do get them. Maybe not as often as I like, but enough to stay in the dance. But I steer clear of the kinky stuff. Life is complicated enough without that. I generally find that the more kinky a woman is the more kookie she is, and my life is full enough of kooky people as it is. Like this woman I needed to stay on the right side of if I was to get out of here alive. I knew she had said no, but I also knew that was just an opening ploy. She would help me in some way. I hoped.

So we talked about other things. Small talk is difficult in our profession. *How are the kids? Don't know – if I go home there is a warrant out for my arrest. How's work? Can't say, it's classified.* But we managed. We told war stories about old campaigns. I enjoyed chewing the fat, but I have to say my stories were funnier than

La Donna's. And hers featured a level of sadism that I try to avoid. If someone has to die I believe I should show them the respect of doing it quickly.

An hour passed and the second bottle, which had appeared mysteriously as the first emptied, was down to half. La Donna pushed her chair back.

"I think it is time to check in on lover boy."

"What's the deal there?" I asked. "Do you just tease him like that all night?"

"Until the main show."

I raised an eyebrow, and she went on.

"Did you notice the webcam on the bedside locker?"

I hadn't.

"That's connected to his home computer. He's on a night-long Skype call to his wife. She's out at work now, but when her shift ends she'll notice the open computer and she'll begin to watch. And that is when the main show begins."

It took me a moment to process that, then the penny dropped. She was going to rape him live on webcam with his wife watching. No wonder the guy looked so uncomfortable. I had thought his reluctance was part of their game. Now I understood. I had underestimated how twisted she was.

She smiled, like a little schoolgirl presenting her daddy with a Father's Day poesy.

"His wife is not in on the game?" I asked, already knowing the answer.

"She's a player. She just doesn't know it yet. When I start I will hook up my laptop so that I can look into her eyes as I do it. The feeling is so much more intense."

"You've done this before?"

"Not often. It's a holiday treat for myself. Who has the time the rest of the year?"

I leaned back in my chair.

"How did you pick him?"

"He picked himself. I was at the bar and he tried to pick me up. I let him. When I knew he was married I knew we had to play the game. Don't worry, he was as into it as I was. He held his hands out for the cuffs. Don't look so disapproving. We're consenting adults."

"And he consented to the webcam?"

"Cherie, you are very innocent. I put the webcam in after I had him secured. I suspect that might have been a deal breaker for him."

I suspected she was right. The poor sucker must be in an absolute panic. Sure, he was a bit of a prick messing around behind his wife's back. But this was almost certainly going to cost him his marriage. What if they had kids? I have a conscience. But I am also human. I didn't like the guy. His wife deserved better. Perhaps this was karma and the universe was just clearing out the garbage. None of my business.

So I let her go up the stairs to her chained sacrifice and I got in a quick coffee to counteract the effects of the glasses of champagne. I strongly suspected that La Donna could drink me under the table and I wanted to end this night upright. I also took a moment to open the wallet I had lifted from the big guy earlier. I know I was going to ask La Donna for money at the end of the evening, but I wanted to be able to cover the bar tab before that. Call it male pride. If the wallet was short I reckoned I had a few minutes to slip out and roll a drunk. I wouldn't feel good about that, but a drunk was now the only ATM open to me. Luckily the wallet was full. Even better, his bank card had the PIN scrawled across it with a sharpie. Some people take no security precautions. If I was a less honest man...

But I couldn't use his card because once I used it the bank's security systems would ping my location. However, his driver's licence might be useful. I slipped the money and licence into my pocket went to the toilet, discretely disposing of the wallet in a trash can once I was out of sight.

I was back at the table, the coffee mug gone and a half-filled glass in front of me, when she reappeared. As she entered the bar she was adjusting her lipstick and I didn't want to think what had smeared it. She pecked me on the cheek and sat down opposite me.

"Short show."

"She's not home yet. It will be another hour. Time enough for you to get me drunk."

She raised her glass and we clinked in a silent toast.

"You never told me what you are doing in Dubrovnik," I said.

"Purely pleasure. I am on holidays for a week."

"And why Dubrovnik?"

I had only been here since afternoon and already I was more than anxious to get out of here. She smiled.

"The cops here are useless. When I pick a location for my games that is an important consideration. One of the most important. You want to pick a place where the game can proceed without a referee intervening. If there are complaints, nothing will be done."

She had that right. I know from my work that once you cross the old Iron Curtain all rules are flexible. A couple of notes of foreign currency could open a lot of doors. Minor indiscretions could be overlooked. I suppose the kidnap and rape of a man who was half consenting could count as a minor indiscretion. Back in Italy it would not be overlooked. And her bosses might not relish the attention on one of their chief enforcers. Dubrovnik made sense.

"Sex tourism," I said.

"Of a kind," she replied.

"Do you do it often?"

"Maybe once a year, when the urge hits."

"And do the guys ever complain afterwards?"

She looked at me oddly. For a while she said nothing and I became painfully aware of the sounds in the bar around me. It was now just past eleven and the joint was as packed as it could be. A couple of elderly men with moustaches were playing cards on one table. A group of young men were talking too loudly and not handling their beer at another table, occasionally bursting into snatches of last year's British pop hits. A couple were having a low but insistent argument two tables away. The bar itself was thronged, with the two servers constantly on the move. I am trained to notice such things, but I wasn't focused. I was looking at La Donna and a slow realisation was dawning.

Then she confirmed it.

"Darling, do you understand the concept of a game? There are winners and there are losers. I win, he loses."

"But I thought..."

"Oh yes, he gets his moment of release. That is his consolation prize. Then I claim my prize."

She sat back with a distant smile on her face. Taking her time, she reached into the pack and drew out a cigarette. She lit it then blew smoke at the ceiling with a sigh.

"After he has come I sit on his face," she said. "I look his woman straight in the eye through the computer and I grip his head tightly between my thighs. I time it so that he has a full breath in his lungs. Then I squeeze. If I time it right – and I will – he will squirm for two minutes, maybe three. His head will jerk convulsively between my legs as he struggles to draw a breath and I will have the most delicious orgasm."

She blew a ring of smoke across the table.

"In two hours' time that fucker upstairs will be dead. And he will die with a smile on my face."

TEN

That was a conversation killer. It dropped right on the table in between us and I couldn't think of a thing to say. Not a single thing.

"Shocked?" she asked.

Yes – and no. As I said, I have a history with La Donna.

"Well I guess that gets rid of the problem of witnesses," I said eventually.

"Don't be a hypocrite. You kill people for a living."

That's a blunt job description. I prefer to think of myself as meeting out justice to those beyond the reach of the more legitimate agencies, a sort of caped crusader without the cape. But I am willing to accept that I am delusional in that.

"I don't kill for fun," I pointed out.

"If you haven't tried it, how do you know you won't enjoy it?"

Sometimes you come up with an unanswerable argument. So I changed the topic.

"My sister is making a porno."

But, because she wasn't, that topic didn't last too long. It was difficult to go back to war stories knowing what was upstairs waiting for her and knowing what she was going to do. I had accepted in my head that the guy was an asshole who deserved the bad karma that was going to shit down on him with a vengeance, but I had assumed the bad karma would involve an encounter with a furious wife, sometimes sleeping alone on the couch and perhaps a frying pan being slapped over his head if she was volatile, as many around the Mediterranean are. Did he really deserve death for infidelity?

But then I thought, if he is unfaithful to his wife he probably fiddles his taxes and cons his customers and alters his expenses sheet. It all adds up. And it wasn't my business. My business was getting out of Mostar. And I hadn't got very far so far.

La Donna solved the problem of conversation. She licked her lower lip in a way that might have been seductive a few hours earlier and smiled at me.

"We could go upstairs and do it on the bed beside him while we are waiting for his wife. Give him a sort of floor show to get him excited before the main event. "

She saw the look on my face and added: "Don't worry – you will be out of there before his wife comes home and tunes in. The main event is a private performance and she won't see your face. It doesn't matter what he sees because he won't be telling anyone."

Why not? La Donna exudes kinky sexuality. I hadn't seen any action in quite a while. And I was betraying no one. I am not in a relationship, so there was no one at home to be let down. I had never done it in front of an audience before, but I am a confident guy. I didn't anticipate any performance anxiety.

I sipped the champagne and considered my choices. The guy upstairs seemed to have limited options. He could die with a smile on his face or a scream. She had her mind made up and I knew I couldn't talk her out of it. And I didn't know him and didn't really care. People die all the time. It is the grand jackpot we all play for and eventually win. He was going to cash out tonight.

That accepted, I could sit here and drink by myself. I could go out for a long walk and come back when it was over. Coming back was a certainty. I needed her help. Or I could trot upstairs for what I knew would be a very memorable encounter. I was beginning to feel a little randy. How enjoyable could it be with him staring at me? Hey, I have done some pretty horrible things in my life. I would get through.

Thus reasoned my rational mind. But behind that a little voice niggled. If I let events run their natural course would the guy upstairs qualify as collateral damage? Not really, since it was nothing to do with me either way. And yet... could I just walk away?

"I need to hit the head and freshen up," I said. "Give me ten minutes."

"You could have put that more tastefully," she said.

"Sorry. I need to freshen up, brush my teeth, make myself beautiful for you."

She smiled.

I did need to hit the head. Too many coffees and too much alcohol in a day will do that to you. I am not a handsome guy so vanity has never been one of my vices. She could take me as she found me in terms of hair and oral hygiene. But she could wait for me; there was work to be done.

I waited in the toilet until a big man was leaving and I came out the door behind him, slipping discretely to the side as I did so. There was no need for the precaution. She wasn't looking in my direction. She was too busy flirting with a guy at the bar. I hoped he wasn't married and into kinky games.

From the bar I made my way to the door leading to the bedrooms. Once I was out of the public area I could drop any pretence at precaution. Speed was what mattered. The empty rooms hadn't been rented, which helped. There was no need for silence. But La Donna's door was still locked and that would slow me down.

There are three ways to open a locked door. The first is familiar to everyone from cop shows. You stand back and kick, or run at it with your shoulder. Here's a newsflash; it only works on the cop shows. And it hurts. No thanks.

The second option is to pick the lock. This is not as easy as it sounds. Everyone thinks you get a bit of wire or a hair clip and jiggle it around a bit. Here's the scoop on that. They are called locks because they are designed to stay locked. If they popped open from a little poke of wire, they would not have caught on. To pick a lock you need two things, not one. You do use a wire or thin metal blade to jog the tumblers up and down, but you also need a tensioner to turn the lock while you are doing that. Without the tensioner the lock will rust apart decades before you can open it. Luckily I had a good set of picking tools, including a range of tensioners. I keep them in my backpack. But my backpack had been destroyed in a bomb attack in Mostar.

That left the third way.

Certain types of door can be opened by forcing a credit card down the crack between the door and the jam, forcing the latch back into the lock and allowing the door to swing free. This isn't a very practical method for a few reasons. The main reason is that credit cards are made of plastic, while locks are brass or iron. So you are more likely to destroy your credit card than gain entry. But with the right door that was still a viable option. This was the right door. The second thing is that you must be on the side that the door opens on to. If the door opens into a room, you won't open it from outside. But many hotels and guest houses, including this one, had doors that open on to the corridor so that they can make the rooms even smaller and squeeze more of them in.

I took off my right shoe. My shoes are very good quality, leather uppers and a composite sole. They are steel toed, which is a bit of an anomaly for stylish shoes but great in a fight. Some of my business cards describe me as an engineer and if anyone asks I do site inspections, which explains the reinforced footwear. One reason for the steel caps is that they explain away the beep as I walk through airport security. The security check shows up the steel, and I am passed through. No one has ever checked the shoes properly. Which is just as well.

I began to work at the back of the heel of my shoe and it only took a moment to pull out the three-inch carbon steel blade. It was a wide blade, more than an inch across at the base and tapering to a sharp point. One edge was serrated, the other honed to a very sharp edge. It was not a weapon, though I suppose you could have used it as one in an emergency. It was a multi-purpose tool. Tonight I was going to use it to open a door.

I worked the blade into the crack between the frame and the door just above the bolt and wedged it down as tightly as possible, the tip of the blade behind the bolt. When it was as near perfectly placed as I could get it, I took my shoe and used it as a hammer, bringing the heel down sharply on the base of the blade. It took two blows, but on the second I felt the bolt give enough and I jerked the door out. Thirty seconds from start to finish. Suck on that, Houdini. I looked into the small room. The poor jerk on the bed was staring at the open door with a look of absolute panic plastered across his pale features. He was screaming, but I couldn't hear him because he was gagged. No sound came out despite his best efforts.

After a few moments he realised that I was on my own. He stopped screaming but the look of panic didn't leave his face. Quickly I put a finger to my lips and glared at him, trying to make him understand. I nodded my head and he nodded back at me, so I put one hand on the gag, a finger still on my lips.

"No noise. Blink if you understand."

It took a few seconds but then he blinked.

"If you do make noise I'll cut off your dick and make you eat it."

He blinked furiously. Gingerly I eased the gag off his mouth, pulling it down towards his throat. He breathed out heavily and his body seemed to relax, slumping into the mattress. Then he tried to struggle up against the ropes that bound him. The look of panic was back on his face. He was frantically trying to jerk his head towards the end of the bed. I turned to look and understood. He was still on camera.

When I snapped the laptop closed and pulled the USB cable out disconnecting the webcam, he smiled with relief.

"Thank you," he whispered. "Now you can kill me. It doesn't matter, so long as Maria doesn't watch."

Ah – true love. He was willing to play around behind her back, but he wanted to spare her the misery of seeing his true nature. Who am I to judge? If I am wrong in my atheism St Peter is only going to sneer at me when I arrived at the pearly gates. I turned back to him and tried to match his smile.

"No one is going to kill you. Not tonight anyway," I said. "I am going to release you and you are going to get as far away from here as you can before she finds out."

As an afterthought I added: "And if you report this to the police I will personally cut your chest open and pull out your heart."

He nodded his understanding. From his heavily accented tone and the fact that he took his time composing sentences I knew his English was not perfect, but fear can do wonders for comprehension. He had no difficulty getting my drift.

"No police," he confirmed. "Out of Dubrovnik. Out of Croatia. She never see me again. Hokey dokey, no problem. I just go."

Sure, if it wasn't for the handcuffs. He saw my glance and understood.

"The thing by the bed," he said.

It took a moment for me to work out that the thing by the bed was the bedside locker. Why don't they teach Europeans a bit more English in school? I am sure he could ask the same question – why hadn't I studied Croatian? But we were making progress. There was a small drawer on the locker and I pulled it open. Unbelievably she had left the keys there. That was careless, and lucky. I could have picked the locks on the cuffs but it would take time. I could have forced them open but it would take even more time and would hurt the guy I was rescuing. So I took the breaks I was given and used the key. I popped both cuffs and he sat up on the bed, rubbing his wrists. He would be sore for a few days, but unless he had struggled and damaged some of the small bones he would get over it quickly.

While he tried to restore the circulation to his hands I went to the end of the bed and undid the ropes binding his ankles.

He grinned at me.

"She never see me again. Hokey dokey, I go."

But he wasn't going. He was just sitting there, rubbing his hands and trying to restore his circulation. I couldn't give a fig for his circulation. I knew La Donna was downstairs. The black widow spider who was going to devour her mate.

"Pull on some clothes, man," I hissed.

He looked at me and suddenly seemed to realise that there was some urgency in the current situation.

"My clothes..."

"Where did she leave them?"

Wouldn't you know it? She had left the key lying around but we couldn't find his clothes. I suspected she had taken them downstairs and put them in one of the bins behind the tavern.

In the morning the bin would be emptied and the evidence would be gone. I could have gone down and looked but time was ticking ominously away. Instead, I opened a drawer and took out lacy black panties and threw them to him. He looked at them in disbelief.

"How do I explain to Maria that I wear another woman's knickers?"

Good question. I had a better one.

"How do you explain to Maria that you are dead?"

This was an unanswerable argument, and he pulled on the panties. We were both thankful that La Donna didn't go for G-strings. The panties were a stretch on him and I wasn't sure about the black lace trim. But it was better than nothing. I tossed him one of her sweaters and as far as I was concerned he was dressed. It was up to him to explain his lack of a trousers once he was clear of the building.

"Now go," I hissed.

He nodded, grabbed my hand and pumped gratefully, then pushed past me out the door. I had to grab him by the shoulders.

"The window," I said. "She could come up the stairs."

We were on the second floor and he didn't like the drop. But eventually he exited that way. It helped that I manhandled him out. I held his wrists and lowered him as far as I could, but when I let go he still had almost two metres to go. He dropped like a stone, hit the ground with his bare feet, yelled an obscenity that I didn't need to speak Croatian to understand, then limped out of my life.

Now I had to get back downstairs before La Donna became suspicious.

ELEVEN

I needn't have worried. She was still flirting with the guys at the bar and barely seemed to register my return. It was like watching moths at a light bulb. I knew that if any of them got too close they would be badly burnt. But she had the chemistry; they found her irresistible. How easy it must have been for her to have got her man upstairs and naked on the bed.

The bottle wasn't empty yet. There comes a time in the night when you should know you have overindulged and should leave a bottle without feeling the urge to empty it. But I have some Irish blood in me and the few ounces of champagne were looking reproachfully at me. I swear it is true. I couldn't leave them on their own. Much wants more and even though I had drunk a bit more than I normally would I still tipped the bottle by the neck and guzzled the last drops. Perhaps it was for courage.

"Hey," La Donna said, "You've emptied my bottle."

"I can get another," I offered.

That would have been ideal. Another bottle, another hour before she discovered who was not waiting for her upstairs. Maybe I could drink her into a stupor and she would never find out. Yeah, and maybe the Ayatollah and the Saudi king would share a bacon butty.

For a moment she was tempted. "Maybe later," she said after

further thought. "First, we will have some fun."

I doubted it but didn't see how I could put off the moment without triggering the fire alarm. Shit, why hadn't I thought of that? It would have been so much easier than what I had actually done. Too late now.

"The night is young. I can get another bottle and we can sit here and allow the anticipation to build up. Call it foreplay. Then we can go upstairs and really have fun. We meet so seldom. Why rush it? A woman as beautiful as you is like an expensive gift. You don't rip the paper off like a child at Christmas. You peel it off carefully, layer by layer, unfolding the wonders at your leisure. Sit down and let me pour you a glass."

"You smooth-talking Casanova. Don't you know that is the sort of talk that makes a woman feel all tingly in all the right places? Now I want to go straight upstairs."

The story of my life; when I want to talk a girl into bed I am laughed at and when I want to sweet talk one out of bed, she practically rapes me. But if it had to be faced, sooner was as good as later. I did my best impression of a lascivious smile and stepped from the table towards her.

"After you, my lady."

She smiled sweetly and walked towards the stairs. I followed her. Common sense told me I should walk the other way, and at a rate that would make an Olympic athlete jealous. But I still needed her help so I was going to ride out the storm. A strategy was forming in my head. When in doubt, lie.

We reached the corridor and she stopped at her door. It was

closed and locked. I am never careless about the details. I had managed to leave no traces of my B&E. She took out her key and I watched as she inserted it in the lock, turning it. There was a click and she pulled the door out. She turned and smiled at me.

"Let's give him a show he will remember for the rest of his short life."

She turned back and entered the room. Time seemed to slow down as I waited for her reaction. There was a moment of silence that seemed to stretch forever. She twisted round and her face was white. She seemed to have aged a decade.

"What's wrong?" I asked.

She stepped aside and I walked into the room.

I did a double-take that Oliver Hardy would have been proud of, then faced to her.

"Where is he? What have you done?"

"He was here when I checked an hour ago. He was tied up securely."

She pointed to the handcuffs still attached to the bedposts. They were closed, as if he had managed to wriggle his hands free. I had closed them after releasing him. Like I say, I don't forget the details. You live and die on details.

"Did you snap them on tight?" I asked, to reinforce the message.

"Tight enough to hurt. This wasn't my first rodeo."

I began to search the room. She looked at me like she might have looked at some dead thing her cat had left on the kitchen floor.

"Do you really think he is hiding in the closet? This is not a cheap farce."

"He can't have gone far. We can find him. It's only been about forty-five minutes since you were up with him. Assume he waited ten minutes to make sure you were really gone. That's thirty-five minutes. Then it would have taken several minutes to work both his hands free. You know that. It's not easy, even if you know what you are doing. And once he had worked his hands free, he had to undo the feet, find his clothes and then sneak out without being seen. He can't have more than ten minutes on us. We'll get him back."

She looked at me, and I could see the hope in her face. It was struggling with the despair. I stepped towards her, reaching out. Then she stepped past me and opened the bedside locker. It's the details that kill you in the end.

TWELVE

She moved so fast it was a blur. One moment she was looking into the empty drawer, the next she was facing me, a look of cold fury on her face. She drew her hand back and slapped me across the face, hard. She was wearing a ring and I could feel the flesh tear, the bead of blood begin to roll down my cheek as the sharp sting of the blow made my head spin.

Of course, I had seen it coming. I am a pro, and you don't catch me that easily. But as I said, I have a code. And part of the code – a bonkers part if you ask me – is that if a woman wants to slap me, I take it. If she had tried for a second one I would have blocked it and spanked her. But she got the first one on the house.

I put a hand up to my face and rubbed gingerly. God, it hurt. A slap is never devastating. It won't knock you out the way a punch to the point of the jaw or the side of the temple will. But it hurts a hell of a lot more than a punch. More than once I have slapped a guy in a bar fight and got the knockout punch in while he deals with the pain and disorientation.

"What was that for?" I asked, still trying to keep up the pretence.

"Why?"

"Did you think I would just sit there and let you kill him?"

"That's what we do. We are killers."

"I'm not a killer. I am a bounty hunter. I bring them back

alive if they want them alive. Dead if they want them dead.
But that's business and there's a reason for it. You were going
to kill that bastard just for your own sick pleasure. There's a
line, and you crossed it."

She looked daggers at me, but I held her gaze and didn't back
down. After a minute she turned away.

"I have to get out of here now," she said.

"He's not going to talk," I assured her. "He ran from here
like a frightened rabbit and I don't think he'll stop running
until he has three countries between you and him. He's
terrified and he knows that if there is an investigation his wife
will find out what he was up to. So you're safe."

She had to believe that because I still hoped she would help
me out.

She paced for a few minutes then turned to me with a
resigned smile.

"It would have been a great night. I've been working so hard
and I really needed the release. And you have screwed it all up
for me. But there is always Plan B."

She walked right up to me and stroked my face gently. It
wasn't stinging anymore, but now I could feel a tingle as her
fingers danced lightly across my skin. I could feel a flutter in
my stomach as her vivid blue eyes bore into mine. I could also
feel the beginning of a flutter somewhere lower.

And then she kneed me in the balls, hard.

The following morning I woke up with a blinding headache.
It felt as if Michael Flatley was running rehearsals for *Lord*

of the Dance inside my skull and some of the dancers were out of step. Badly out of step. The sunlight filtering into the room grated on my eyeballs like sandpaper. I closed my eyes quickly and began to run a quick scan across my body. Nothing seemed broken and I wasn't running a fever. Aside from the headache and general soreness – and a tenderness in my nether regions that could not be ignored – I seemed to be fine. But I couldn't move. My arms and legs would not respond to orders from my foggy brain. Was I paralysed?

It took a moment, but I figured it out. I was tied to the bed, spread-eagled. So I stopped struggling and tried to relax. I began with a breathing exercise, trying to get my blissful mindfulness to kick in. But it wasn't working today. My head was pounding. How much had I had to drink the night before? I hadn't had a hangover like this since my student days.

As I tried to clear my head thoughts kept intruding, driving the calmness away. Fleeting images and dreamlike sequences flashed before me and I went with them. Slowly I began to remember the night before. It had begun with a kick in the balls. I remembered doubling over and hitting the bed as La Donna swept my foot from under me with a perfectly timed jujitsu move. Before I could begin to react she was on me, cuffing my wrist to the bed. After that I was at her mercy.

Somehow I knew she wasn't going to kill me. I had spoiled her plans but we had a history and our history would not end like that. So did I began to go along with her? My recollection was shaky through all the fog in my head. But I know she cuffed my other hand to the other bedpost, then removed my trousers. She must have done, because I certainly wasn't wearing them now. Then she must have secured my legs.

I would love to say I had an earth-shattering night, but I simply don't know. I do recall an argument about the state of my equipment. She wasn't satisfied. I tried to blame her. After all she was the one who had kicked me.

I have a recollection of her later popping a blue pill into my mouth, which I didn't want to swallow. She had poured water into my mouth, then slammed my chin up to close it. She pinched my nose and it was a case of swallow or choke, so I swallowed. There was a second pill. The blue one was Viagra, of course. She had probably used that on her earlier victim too, so that she could play with him when all his instincts were screaming that this was no turn on. So what was the second tablet? Then I remembered that in the drawer with the cuff keys was a box of painkillers, Tramadol. The only reason I remembered was that Tramadol is not a common European medicine. Then it came to me —it is often used to dull feelings and prolong performance. She had really wanted something to play with.

There were other pills – there had to be. I totted up what I had drank the previous evening and it came nowhere near explaining the strength of the hangover. Or the fact that I couldn't remember much of what had happened. It could have been a tranquillizer, or something more sinister.

What did it matter? I was still stuck to the bed. I was pinned there, like an insect in an entomologist's sample tray.

THIRTEEN

Getting out of handcuffs without a key can be tricky. The best way to do it is to distract the person putting on the cuffs. Most people don't realise it, but a handcuff doesn't lock securely until you push the spike at the end of the key into a small hole in the locking mechanism. If someone is not used to cuffing people, or if you distract them at the right time, then all it takes is a bit of physical force and the cuffs pop off. But one tug told me that La Donna had not been distracted. These cuffs were secure all right.

That left two options. The first was to pick the lock. How? Both hands were secured to different sides of the bed. That left one option, and it wasn't a pleasant one. I would have to physically rip my hand through the cuff and out. It would hurt, it would damage the hand, and it would take time.

Luckily I started with two advantages. The first is that even after a kick in the balls our instincts are still firmly in place. I knew I would have tightened my wrist as she cuffed me, slightly puffing up the muscles. This meant that they were not as tightly on as she thought. The second is that I had done this before, many times. It is one of the things we prepare for in the hopes we will never have to do it for real.

There was no point in tugging wildly. This had to be done slowly and systematically. I began by pushing up in the bed as far as possible to give myself a tiny bit more room. Then I squeezed the thumb and little finger of my left hand together as tightly as possible. I pushed my hand back behind the bedpost then pulled it slowly forward, so that the edge of the cuff caught on the metal of the bed. This gave me something to pull against. Now it was a matter of pulling slowly and steadily. As I pulled I felt the cuff tighten over the base of my thumb. When I had pulled it up as far as it could go on that side I turned my wrist slightly and began pulling the cuff over the base of my little finger. The first two pulls gave me about half an inch. The next pull gave me far less as the cuff reached the thicker part of my hand. At this point a pound of butter would have helped enormously, and to try to control the increasing pain I imagined a beautiful redhead leaning over me and gently performing that unction. In my mind I could sense her fingers kneading the soft butter into my skin, and could feel the cuff slide over rather than ripping the flesh.

It took a few minutes and the pain as the cuff slowly passed over the first joint of my thumb was excruciating. But in the end the cuff cleared that point. The first joint of the little finger was less painful. Once it was past those two joints all I had to do was maintain the pressure, move my wrist to keep the pull even and do it gently so as not to do more damage. My hand slipped free.

I took a moment then wet my tongue and kicked my fingers. I applied this moisture to my other hand, and used my left hand to pull the cuff over my right. This was a lot quicker. The moisture helped and the fact that I was pulling with another hand rather than pushing against a bedpost also helped. In

a few minutes both hands were free and I sat up in the bed
rubbing my wrists. The foot bindings were now a piece of cake
and soon I was sitting at the side of the bed, buck naked. Time
to get dressed.

Easier said than done. The bitch had stolen my clothes.

It didn't take long to toss the bedroom; there was nothing
to wear. I did find a letter, though, addressed to me. It was
written in an ornate feminine style on scented lavender paper.
It was left on a chair well away from the bed, where she knew I
couldn't reach it. I smiled as I picked it up and began to read.

'My darling Eli,

*'Thanks for last night. And sorry I had to run this morning. I did give
you a kiss before I left, but you didn't wake up. Rohypnol does that.'*

I knew it wasn't the champagne!

'I hope your head is not too bad, Cherie. But you deserved it.

*'It is not likely you are reading this letter but if you are, you are a
better man that I thought. More likely you are lying on the bed struggling
against the chains and ropes and cursing me. Don't curse too much – I
will help you. I have a plan.*

*'I will be back later to untie you. If you are reading this try to return
to the hotel by six. I will tell you all.*

'You were magnificent last night.

'Hugs and kisses, your Donna.'

I tossed the letter on the bed and checked the corridor
outside. No one was around, so it was safe to walk out naked.
I broke into one room on the corridor and found nothing.
I broke into the second and was lucky enough to find a suit
that fitted me. It was old-fashioned and I looked like an east

European peasant in his Sunday best, but at least no one was going to arrest me for indecency. Then I left the hotel and disappeared into the warren of streets outside. No point in remaining where La Donna thought I was. I trusted her about as much as I would trust a shark in a feeding frenzy.

FOURTEEN

How do you kill time in a town like Dubrovnik? Stupid question – it's one of the prettiest towns in Europe. And if I was a tourist I would have loved it. But I wasn't a tourist. I was a bounty hunter with a price on my head, and that makes the difference. I had a crick in my neck from looking over my shoulder. Now that La Donna knew I was here, who else might know? It's not as if I didn't trust her, even though I didn't. It's just that I am always acutely aware of a quote from Benjamin Franklin: 'Three can keep a secret if two of them are dead'.

But if you can't trust your friends, no matter how odd and twisted, who can you trust?

I decided to go to the oldest part of the town, inside the ancient walls. The streets were very narrow here and all motorised vehicles were banned. If I was hunted down at least it would be a level playing pitch. They would be on foot, I would be on foot. They would be armed with a small gun, I would be armed... Hang on, I wouldn't be armed. It was not a level playing pitch. I was a moving target. I slipped a steak knife from a pavement café table into my pocket as I passed. It was not enough but better than nothing.

After an hour of aimless wandering I was reasonably sure I was not being followed or observed. I could spend the rest of the day wondering, or I could try to relax and go with the flow. Be in the moment, my mindfulness teacher would have said. The moment called for a strong coffee. And I had picked up enough change in the bedrooms I had raided to at least afford that. I chose a café with small tables out in front, facing the sea. I sat with my back to the wall, both approaches in full view, and ordered a cappuccino. In Europe you can have a cappuccino up to midday and not appear a hick. After that it is espresso all the way, but they will serve you an americano without looking at you as if you were something scraped from the bottom of a shoe.

I sipped the strong coffee and considered my options. There were none really. I could trust La Donna to come up with something, if you could call that an option. Or I could try to leave Croatia without a passport. It is not part of the Schengen Area. Most European countries have abolished passport control at their borders. But Croatia was one of the few not in on the deal. And so was Britain. I couldn't get out of where I was or into where I wanted to be without showing paper. I reached into my pocket for my phone and came out empty-handed. Of course. She had taken my phone with my clothes. She really wasn't being much of a friend.

I called the waiter back and asked him if the establishment had a phone I could use. He looked at me sceptically but, eventually, when I assured him it was a local call, he retreated, returning a few minutes later with a handset. I waited until he was gone, then keyed in the number. Not quite local, but it would show on the bill as local and the other end would pick up the charges.

The phone rang twice, then he picked up.

"You prick," he said.

"And a good morning to you too, Bill," I replied.

"You fucking prick. It's four in the morning. It is never a good morning when someone rings you at four. You know what people do at four? They sleep. I was asleep. My woman was asleep. You're lucky you didn't wake her up. If I hadn't got to the phone in time..."

"What's up, honey?" I could hear a faint female voice in the background. "Put the phone down. I'm trying to sleep."

"Shit – you've done it now. You've woken her."

There were sounds of movement over the phone, a few curses, then his voice came back clear.

"Now I'm up and standing in the kitchen in my bare feet. This had better be good."

"Actually I had forgotten the time difference, Bill," I admitted sheepishly. "It's mid-morning here and I just thought it was the same in Langley."

"I'm not in Langley now. I'm at home," he said peevishly.

"And where do you live?"

I had him there. He lived in Langley, three kilometres from where he worked. It was a lovely leafy suburb full of Washington types.

"In Jefferson," he snapped.

I had forgotten the separation. He had moved on quickly if there was already a new woman sharing his bed. But now was not the time to probe that. If I ever got home I could get all the dirty details.

"Are you on your way home?" he asked with a sigh.

"Not quite," I admitted. "It hasn't been an easy journey. I'm still in Dubrovnik. I have no phone, no money, no weapons and no papers. And I am in a cheap suit I stole this morning. And a set of La Donna's panties. But don't ever admit that I told you that."

He laughed.

"Was it a good night at least?"

"I have no idea. She fed me a roofie."

He laughed again and I was starting to find it irritating.

"It's not funny. I have a splitting headache and my balls hurt."

"Are her knickers that tight?"

"She tried to kill a man last night."

That stopped the laughing.

"When I got there she had a man tied to her bed, naked. She was going to kill him on a webcam with his wife looking on."

"Wow – that's her? Fascinating."

"What the fuck do you mean, fascinating? She was going to kill him for some sort of sexual kick."

"Yes, they usually do. Interpol's profile has her down as a sexual deviant. It's quite a common motivation among serial killers. They reckoned a dominant woman, single, probably well-adjusted but solitary, and holding a stressful and high-status job. Would mafia hit-man count as a high-status job?"

"Did you know about her?"

"No – her name never even occurred to me. But I can see how she fits. Is she going to help you?"

"Hang on – you can't just say fascinating and move on. Why

does Interpol have a profile of her."

"Not of her specifically," Bill said. "They have a profile of
the Webcam Killer. You've heard of the Webcam Killer?"

No I hadn't.

"She's been around for a few years now. Six confirmed kills.
Interesting MO. She lures guys who are on the road – truckers,
salesmen, that sort of man – to a cheap hotel or apartment and
she ties them to a bed. Then she sets up a webcam connected
to their home computer through Skype or one of the other
messaging services..."

"I know how she works. I was in the room."

"Did you see the kill?" He sounded genuinely fascinated, as
if I was describing a rare bird I had spotted in a forest or an
exhibit at the museum that he had missed.

"I rescued the guy."

"Oh." Did he sound disappointed? "I suppose it was the
right thing to do."

"So what now?" I asked.

"Is she going to help you get out of Croatia?"

"I mean, do I hold her for Interpol, or do we just pass on the
information and let them handle it?"

"How many of those roofies did she feed you? I don't work
for Interpol. I work for the CIA. You work for yourself. It's
none of our business. So you stay on the right side of that
mad bitch and you use her to get out of Croatia and you keep
your mouth shut. Capeesh? I know that offends against your
code, but we're not boy scouts here. When you get home we
can send an anonymous tip to Interpol if you insist. But not

until then."

"What if she doesn't help me?"

"Don't worry. I have a Plan B," said Bill. "I have a week leave due to me and I am flying to Rome today. You'll cover the cost. I have a yacht chartered out of Pescara and I will sail across to Dubrovnik. I should get there the day after tomorrow. If you are still there I will pick you up. If not, I will sail on to Venice and call it a vacation."

"You don't sail," I interrupted.

"My son does."

"Jesus – Ben is just sixteen."

"So I'll take him out of school for a week. No big deal."

"What does Rita say?" Rita was his ex, not the woman in his bed.

"She probably wouldn't approve. But tonight is my night to have him. I'll take him out of school on my way to the airport and she won't find out until he doesn't come home tomorrow evening. Problem solved. It is sometimes easier to ask for forgiveness rather than permission."

That was the stupidest thing I had heard in quite a while – but also one of the most touching. It was a sign of the depth of our friendship that he was willing to do that for me, and I was grateful. Now it was doubly important that La Donna came through for me. I couldn't let him risk his son's life and what was left of his relationship with his ex.

We left it at that and said our goodbyes. I called over the waiter and handed him back the phone and a fistful of coins. Then I turned back to the road. And spotted her.

FIFTEEN

She was walking down the street towards the sea, and if I hadn't been scanning the street I would have missed her. She saw me too. The redhead from Mostar, the one with the legs who didn't have daddy issues. What was she doing here? I had seen her at the airport yesterday morning.

She hesitated when she saw me, then waved uncertainly. There was nothing for it. I waved back.

"I thought I saw you at the airport yesterday," she said.

"I thought the same about you."

I looked at her. She shrugged. "I was meant to fly to Rome to meet my brother, but I got a call that he missed his connection in Dubai. So I have a few days more to kill."

You didn't need to be a detective to work it out.

"Afghanistan?"

"Yes – but how did you know?"

"If he's making a connection through Dubai he is either there or in Australia. Is he military or civilian?"

"I'm not meant to say."

"With that answer you just have said."

We both laughed.

"Can I sit down?"

"Have you got over your daddy issues?" I asked.

"Sorry – but you did look old that day. A lot older than you do today."

"There was dust in my hair. If you had given me a chance I could have shaved fifteen years off my age with a damp cloth."

She sat and I waved the waiter over, calling for two coffees. I was really beginning to stretch my limited supply of coins.

"So what's your story?" she asked.

"A bit embarrassing. Someone lifted my wallet, got most of my money and my passport."

She made a sympathetic noise and put a hand on my arm. It felt good. "Have you been in touch with the embassy?"

I made a non-committal noise and moved my head in a way that could be taken as a nod or a shake.

"What's with the grandfather suit?" she asked, as the waiter laid the coffees on the table.

"I'm having a bit of a run of bad luck. My room was broken into last night and all my clothes stolen. So I borrowed this off the landlord. Actually, that's a lie. I stole it off the landlord. I'm living the renegade life."

From her face I could see she didn't know whether to smile or frown sadly. Then she smiled, and it was glorious. Her face lit up. I had been reserved up to then but her smile opened me up and I grinned back. There was nothing in it. I was just killing time. But killing time in company is more fun than killing time on your own.

"We got off to a bad start a few days ago," she said. "My name is Jelly. I'm a teacher from England. But you knew that from the accent. I'm using the summer holidays to tour around the Med for a month."

There must have been something in the way I looked at

her, because she went on: "Jelly is not my real name. But my brother was a year old when I was born and couldn't say 'Jenny'. And it stuck. Your turn."

"My name is Eli Varrick, my brother can say my name, and I am a professional mountaineer."

"Sure you are."

"Okay," I conceded. "I lead groups of tourists on exotic adventure holidays. But I have been up mountains."

"Any I would recognise?" she asked, sceptically.

"Kilimanjaro, Everest."

"I'm impressed. Did you get to the top?"

"On some. Not the full way on Everest."

"Did you get beyond base camp?"

I shrugged.

"So now you know. I am a chancer," I said. "A dilettante who talks big and leaves the climbing to the experts."

"Always mountains?"

"Oh no. Big wave surfing, up to two metres. Big game hunting. In fact, that's the real reason I am in a borrowed suit. I lost my own in a big poker game last night."

"And an amateur comedian. Don't give up the day job," she laughed.

I was beginning to relax. Boredom is something I hate and I tend to get into trouble when I have too much time on my hands. This woman was growing on me. That is a problem we men tend to suffer from; if you laugh at our jokes, we will fall for you. We are easily manipulated that way. I wasn't falling for her, but I was certainly thinking of how to spend a few hours in her company. I could justify it by pretending it was to keep myself from doing something stupid on my own.

But if this was going to work, we had to be straight with each other. By that I mean, she had to be honest with me. I wasn't about to tell her I worked as a bounty hunter. It is best to keep some mystery. But I needed to know about her.

I looked at her, my smile fixed broadly on my face.

"As long as we are being honest," I said, "tell me what you really do. Because you are no teacher."

Her face froze for a moment. It was only a fleeting moment, but I have trained myself to read the micro-expressions that flit across a person's face when they are under pressure. It was there. Then she was smiling at me again. But it took her a full minute to answer me.

"You are right," she said eventually. "But so am I. Yes, I work as a teacher. But I wasn't always one."

"You were military."

"Yes. I did a full ten-year hitch and retired on a modest pension. So I am a teacher now, or at least a teacher's assistant. I'm studying part-time and will be a teacher in the end. The army gave me a grant to study."

I digested that for a moment.

"You only get a grant if you are invalided out. Where did you serve?"

"Two tours of Afghanistan. Near the end of my second tour I signed up for a third. But with two days to go we were on patrol in a hot zone. We thought the insurgents had been cleared out so I guess we weren't being as careful as we should have been. And we had sniper cover too. It seemed to be routine. We were near the end of the patrol, just ten minutes to go. We had turned and were making our way back to the barracks when we saw it. There was a child lying in the middle of the road. The child hadn't been there twenty minutes earlier. She wasn't moving, just a wee thing in a pink cardigan and tatty pants. My OC told us all not to move but I had to go and check on her. I had to see was she alive.

"I ignored the OC and moved forward. The sniper was covering me so I felt safe. I got up to her and she wasn't moving. She can't have been more than six. There were no marks on her and I thought she might be asleep. Or sick. So I turned her over to check. That's when the mine under her body exploded."

She was silent for a moment and took a nervous sip of her coffee.

"Christ, I could do with a beer. I turned her over and she went up like Bonfire Night. Her body shielded me from the worst of the blast, but my lower leg was shattered."

She bent down and pulled up the left leg of her jeans to reveal a shapely calf and skin that was pocked and scarred. "One other soldier had disobeyed the OC and come up to the girl with me. She was on the other side and nothing shielded her. She took the full blast. I was picking parts of her out of my hair for a week."

I made a sympathetic face but said nothing. What can you say to that?

"She was my lover."

Wow. Now I really was speechless. I gently reached across the table and took her hand lightly in mine, squeezing reassuringly. She smiled weakly.

"Any smart comments now?"

"So you're a lesbian? How's that working out for you? I see I struck out for more than daddy issues."

Her smile was rueful and wavering.

"I'm not a lesbian really. I am more straight than anything. But it was the army. I don't know if you know any army types, but they tend to be brainless morons. Your standard grunt is about as attractive as a side of six-week-old beef. I don't think that Linzi and I would have stayed together after we got home, but we would have remained good friends. I lost that. I nearly lost my leg. But they patched me up and sent me to teach school. And now you have the full story."

That put a damper on proceedings. Where do you go from there? There was an awkward silence that stretched. Wisecracking Eli, at a loss for words when a real woman was in pain. Then I noticed behind her a handwritten sign: "Cold beers and gorgeous views. 300 metres."

"You need a beer," I said decisively.

SIXTEEN

I have never known three hundred metres to take so long – or to pass so delightfully. We left the café and followed the handwritten sign, which contained a rough red arrow. We walked up a narrow street, passing the handcarts that are used in the old quarter to make deliveries. We came to a T-junction, with another handwritten sign. But the arrow pointed straight up. We debated left or right and eventually tossed a coin. It came up wrong. Heads, where the direction was tails. So we lost ten minutes before we found another sign. This one had an arrow, but it pointed towards the middle of a fork. It was like a mad treasure hunt and it took thirty minutes to get there. We went up and down narrow streets, crossed shadowy courtyards, found two beautiful plazas and finally arrived at a narrow steep lane that went up along the side of the medieval wall. The wall was huge and dank, its shade giving a welcome break from the heat of the sun.

At the top of the lane we came to one of the old gates of the city, a narrow crack in the wall just wide enough to accommodate a man leading a fully laden horse. The gates had been made deliberately narrow; you did not want a gap that an army could come through. We were able to walk through side by side, which brought me deliciously close to Jelly. I didn't object.

The wall was nearly three metres thick and when we got

through the ground fell sharply beneath us. The vista was magnificent; sapphire blue sea dotted with small boats of all descriptions. In the distance, merging into the heat haze, were the darker shades of the islands. We were on a cliff face. It wasn't sheer, but if you fell you were going the whole way to the sea. Above us, up a rough path, was the establishment offering the cold beer and glorious views. It was the oddest bar I had seen. The main bar was dug into the cliff and had a patio with about eight tables. There were four other smaller patios, some above the bar, some below, spread across the cliff like the nests of sea birds.

We ordered beers, of course, and sat in companionable silence enjoying the spectacle. The beers were cold. The views were gorgeous. The sign had not lied. It was peaceful, apart from the highest nest, which was occupied by a rowdy group of young men and women. I knew the type because I had been one only a few years – or perhaps a decade – earlier. The men were juiced on testosterone, desperate to impress the women. The women were at an age when nothing would impress them. I tuned them out.

"So what's your plan?" Jelly asked eventually.

"I have a friend who is trying to sort me out with papers. Meanwhile, I wait." I lifted my glass. "The waiting is easy."

"If he doesn't sort you out …"

"She," I corrected, and immediately regretted it though I could not have said why.

Jelly looked at me.

"She? Is she cute?"

"It depends on what you are into," I said non-committedly.

She grinned. "Are you sleeping with her?"

God, I hope not. My balls wouldn't stand another night. And I couldn't even remember if I had enjoyed it or not.

Jelly must have seen the look that crossed my face because she smiled broadly.

"Is she that bad?"

I wasn't going to tell her about La Donna. I was under no illusions I had any chance with Jelly, but a man is a man and I play the odds. So the less said about the murderous sex-bomb who had a date with me that evening the better. Instead, I raised a hand for the waiter and ordered a salad. The time passed easily. I don't know exactly how long we spent there, but if memory serves me correctly it was four beers, a salad and a very nice cheesecake. I know we were still chatting easily by mid-afternoon. The rowdy young men and women had been replaced by an American couple who lunched and left, then by a group of late teen boys, too young to drink in some jurisdictions but happily downing the Heineken from their cliff-top eerie. Around three, one of the boys threw himself off the railing and sailed in a graceless arc down the side of the cliff. He hit the sea with a splash and a huge cheer rang up from the tables and from the few people on top of the city walls who could see the jump.

A few minutes later a second guy jumped and within a few minutes it had become the sport of choice in that part of Dubrovnik. The crowd began to grow on the walls as the young men tested their manhood against the challenge. Some jumped gracefully and hit the water with a minimal splash. Some just bombed into the water, shouting as they hit. One or two chanced a dive. The cliff was particularly steep where they were jumping and all cleared the rocks easily. Clearly they knew there was deep water beneath. Jelly and I cheered with the rest and chipped in our scores for the better efforts.

"Ten years ago I would have been right there with them," I said. "I would have been scoring tens with every dive."

"Bullshit, old man," she said. "You would have been holding their towels and praying no one asked you to join in. I know your type. You're a hill walker, not a cliff diver."

"Would you give me a date if I jumped?"

"I can give you a date anyway – 6 June 1945. I have plenty more dates if you want them."

"Seriously."

"If you dive, I'll give you a kiss."

"It will have to do."

I stood up. She was still laughing. It was only a moment to reach the platform from where everyone was jumping and diving. I went to the edge and looked over. I could see the darkness in the sea that had to be the landing area. From up here it looked small enough. For a moment discretion fought with valour and discretion was winning. She was right; I am not a high diver. I do things when my life is at risk but, in general, I am content to sit back and relax with a good book and a glass of single malt. Then one of the teens grinned at me and said something I didn't understand. I looked at him and shrugged, the universal sign language for 'I haven't a clue what you said'.

"Is too dangerous. You kill yourself, old man," he translated.

There it was again, 'old man'. That's my father. That won't be me for another forty years. Without a word, I turned from the edge. The kids laughed. Then I began climbing the side of the cliff, gaining height rapidly. I had spotted a small rock that cropped out from the face about four metres above the nest of tables. That was where I was making for. It wasn't a difficult climb. A tough grade four, borderline grade five. In layman's terms; a rope should be there to secure the climber. But I was never one for rules. I got a hand on the rock outcrop and levered myself upright. It protruded about twenty centimetres, plenty of room for me to stand comfortably. Then I looked down.

The problem was immediately obvious. The guys jumping from the edge of the platform below me had to get out about more than a metre to ensure they hit the water safely. From my perch, I would have to clear three metres or more to be safe. A nine-foot standing jump is not an easy thing. I looked down at the guys on the platform. They were looking up at me, grinning their encouragement. A hush had descended on them, like the hush in a stadium before the champion prepares for the winning jump. I looked down and across to Jelly. She was looking up at me, a curious look on her face.

It was now or never. I should have at least taken off my jacket. I should have removed my shoes. I should have... I bent down quickly, touching my toes. This ensured that my knees were bent enough to provide the push I would need. Then I straightened explosively, throwing my hands forward and springing violently from the rock. I felt the air rush past me and then I was clear of the tables and soaring past the cliff face. Fifteen metres below, the water rushed at me. The cliff shot by only centimetres away. It would be a close thing ...

SEVENTEEN

I hit the water perfectly and came up to cheers and laughter.
I turned towards the shore and Jelly had a strange look on
her face, half smile, half something else. That's the problem
with women. You set out to impress them and then discover
that common sense and reliability can often be as appealing as
displays of machismo. But I felt great, the adrenalin rush lifting
my spirits and helping me forget for a while why I was in this
lovely town with death at my back and the vast emptiness of
the Adriatic to the front.

As I dried off we finished our beers and the bar owner
sent over complimentary ones in acknowledgement of the
highest dive of the day. One was enough for me. I had proved
something, at least to myself, and was content to leave it at
that. The young men continued to leap and we continued to
cheer. The afternoon lingered.

By the time the second beer was killed, my cheap suit had
almost dried out. But my shoes still squelched and I would
probably blister on the walk home. God, how I wanted to get
home.

I got my kiss before we left and I would have got a date too,
I believe, but tonight was for La Donna. If she could get me
out of here...

We walked back through the wall into the old quarter
together, found our way to one of the long streets leading

from the sea up to the new quarter, and paused. We stood awkwardly, not knowing what to say.

"If you're around tomorrow..." I began.

"That would be nice," Jelly said. Then we smiled and turned our separate ways. It would be nice to see her again, but deep down I knew it wouldn't happen. The vague promise to meet up was a polite platitude. Tonight I would get the help I needed and by this time tomorrow I would be long clear of Croatia. I think she knew it too, even if she didn't know the trouble I was in. It was a fleeting contact, like seabirds tossed together on a storm only to be thrown as quickly apart. Special but brief. I walked wistfully away.

I stopped at a small kiosk to buy a take-away coffee. The shade of the afternoon on the damp suit was chilling me and I thought a hot drink as I walked would help. I used my last few coins and got a latte. To hell with European conventions about not having a milky coffee in the afternoon. I had dived the height of a four-storey building. I was invincible. I could drink a latte.

I stepped back on to the street and took a sip. Delicious. I lowered the cup to chest height and walked on. As I reached the top of the street I thought I would turn and see if I could catch one more brief glimpse of the svelte and sexy Jelly. She was probably long gone, but I turned anyway. That turn saved my life.

As I turned, the paper coffee mug in my hand imploded, the hot liquid gushing over my hand. I felt the scalding pain and felt the wisp of a breeze pass over my hand and disappear almost instantly. Instinct took over. Before I could even begin to process what was happening my knees buckled and I fell to the ground as if shot. My body twisted as I fell, my hip hitting the ground at an angle as my body rolled, the fall being taken by my hip, my back and my shoulder in quick succession. Like a paratrooper hitting the ground in the good old days before controlled descent, I collapsed and ended up prone on the pavement without any part of my body taking the brunt of the fall.

I ended up in the gutter, my torso and head between a cart and the pavement, my legs exposed.

My brain began putting together the pieces. There had been no sound, but coffee cups don't explode in your hand like that. And the rush of air past my hand; the only thing that made sense was a bullet. But it had been subsonic. There was no characteristic crack as it punched through the sound barrier. Pistol round? No. The shooter would have had to get too close to me. Beautiful women might distract me, but not that much. I would have noticed. And it would be too risky; he would have to be able to escape after taking the shot.

So a sniper. And a pro, if he had a silenced rifle and the experience to use a reduced velocity round. I didn't move. Lying down in the gutter I presented a smaller target. And if I didn't move, he might think he had hit me. Job done and he would be already up and moving. Although every instinct said run for cover, I forced myself to remain immobile. I began counting the seconds in my head. I would give it two minutes.

The only thing I moved were my eyes. I scanned as much

of the street ahead of me and to my side as I could. I couldn't see anything. Without moving my head it was difficult. I was relying on peripheral vision. Where would I set up the shot? I looked at rooftops and balconies. I looked for open windows.

A man ran up to me and grabbed me by the shoulder. He shook me gently and began jabbering at me in what my brother would have described as 'foreign'. Croatian is a type of foreign I don't speak, but I knew he was asking how I was. The good Samaritan, helping a man who had tripped or had a heart attack. I didn't move. Too early. A second person stopped and bent over me, concern written all over his face.

Then I saw it, the glint of light from a roof about seventy metres away. There was a low parapet on the roof and I couldn't see anyone, only the glint. But I knew what it was all right. In the movies that would have been the sniper fixing his telescopic sight on my prone form. But this was no movie. The sniper was packing up. You never catch the glint before the shot, because the gun is not moving and the sight is fixed firmly on your head or chest. Now the gun was moving and the sun caught the telescopic sight and I saw the flash. In ten seconds he would be on the other side of the roof, probably heading for a fire exit and a waiting motorcycle. He either believed he had hit me or was not willing to risk a shot now that I was surrounded. I waited for the roar of the motor, then remembered that we were in the pedestrianised section of the town. He would be escaping on foot. I might be able to catch him.

And then what? He had the gun. I had a damp suit and

squelchy shoes. This one I had to let go.

The danger was over now. I sat up and smiled weakly at the small group of concerned people who had gathered around me. I reached a hand up and one of them pulled me to my feet. I gingerly put my weight down on my right foot and winced, as if I had tripped and twisted an ankle. A man immediately rushed to support me. I tried again, this time getting my foot under me. I limped off to their murmurs of sympathy.

Once I was around the corner I stopped limping and moved swiftly into the shadows. The stakes had risen considerably now. This morning I thought I was waiting to sneak out of a country without papers. I thought I was broke, weapon-less and safely away from Mostar. Now I knew differently. Whoever had tried to kill me in Bosnia was still on my trail and knew exactly where I was. It was no longer a waiting game. I was the prey and I didn't know who was hunting me. But I knew he was close.

EIGHTEEN

It took me nearly an hour to get back to the hotel. I must have walked every street and alley in the centre of Dubrovnik, many of them twice or three times. I paused, reversed, ran and hid, checked windows for reflections. I dived down behind dumpsters, passed in and out of the walled section twice, ducked into two bars and out back doors and finally went into a restaurant toilet. I got out through the window and climbed a wall. By that stage, I was fairly sure I wasn't being followed. I'm good and if anyone was still on my tail he was very good. No one was that good.

I didn't walk into the hotel. Not tonight. Instead I waited until the street at the rear was empty, then pulled a dustbin under La Donna's window. That left me only about three metres short. Shit. I got a hand on the mounting of the satellite dish and a foot on a drainpipe. Neither was very secure, but I got enough of a boost to get a hand on the windowsill and, once I got that, I was as good as in. Luckily the window was open.

I stripped off the damp clothes and had a shower. I wrapped a towel around my waist and sat on the bed. Then I fell back, put my hands under my head, closed my eyes and lost myself in my mindfulness exercises. Despite all that had happened here last night, despite the shot fired at me this afternoon, I felt safe in the small room. This was La Donna's lair. She scared the hell out of me, but then she would scare the hell out of anyone else in the game too. I was safe – at least until she arrived.

I would like to say that I maintained perfect mindfulness for the next hour but I suspect that I fell asleep. The reason I suspect this is because I was suddenly aware of footsteps in the corridor outside and the sound of a key scratching in the door. I sat up in the bed and looked relaxed when La Donna walked in. She looked stunning, in tight leather trousers and a scarlet blouse that emphasised her cleavage.

"Hi dear. I hope you didn't mind. I forgot to leave you the keys when I left this morning."

"Not a problem," I smiled.

She looked at the end of the bed and grinned broadly.

"You never lost it. So, did you have a good day?"

"I relaxed, saw the sights."

"Really?"

"Of course not," I said. "I have a mad warlord on my tail and no papers to get home. And a mad woman tying me up with cuffs and ropes."

"That was for your own protection."

"And the cocktail of drugs?"

"That was for my amusement."

At least she was honest.

She sat on the bed beside me and ran a finger slowly up my thigh, towards the edge of the towel. My skin tingled. I thought of the list of heavyweight champions since Larry Holmes retired; and nothing more stirred. I don't think she was looking for a reaction, but there was electricity in her touch. I needed to focus. If she helped me, I might make it out in the next day or so. But if she didn't...

"Have you any news on a passport for me?" I asked.

She looked at me ruefully, almost disappointed.

"Straight down to business. No kiss for your lady? I explained to you last night, I am under orders. No one will help you."

"We go back a long way, La Donna."

"We do. And we will talk later. But first, dinner. And put on some clothes."

"Someone took my clothes before she left this morning."

"Nonsense, dear. They are in the case under the bed."

I looked under the bed and there was a rough suitcase, ages old. I pulled it out and inside were my clothes, neatly folded. My wallet was there too, with the money I had taken after the bar fight. And my phone. Everything was in order.

"I must have missed that this morning," I said. And I had missed it for a very good reason; it hadn't been there. Which meant La Donna had returned during the day and knew I had escaped her bindings. She was playing games but, as I said, we have a history and I knew all about her dramatic tenancies. So I went along with it.

Twenty minutes later we strolled down to the bar for dinner as if we didn't have a care in the world. She had steak, served blue, and a salad. I went for the fish. She had red wine. I had water. I wanted to keep my wits about me. After the meal we had a coffee and she had a Grappa. I think she was a bit disappointed I wasn't drinking but, to be honest, I was more concerned about keeping alert and alive than keeping her happy.

Finally she suggested we go for a walk. So we did. We left the hotel and walked about two hundred metres, where we found a deserted bench overlooking a wide street. The whole time my eyes were scanning the buildings around us, but I could see no immediate threats. We sat. No one could overhear us. The time had finally come to talk. But I wouldn't let her have the satisfaction of seeing me worried; I would let her make the running. I sat in silence, outwardly patiently, inwardly in a stew.

"I suppose you'd like to get home?" she finally said.

"No. Dubrovnik is growing on me. I love it here. I might buy an apartment overlooking the harbour and wait out my golden years."

"With your tall brunette?"

That brought me up. How did she know? Had I been followed all day?

"I have my sources," she grinned. "Let's just say a little bird told me about your little bird."

"Did the little bird tell you how to get me a passport?" I asked. There, I had done it. I had broken first and brought up the topic we were both here to discuss.

She grinned.

"You aren't listening. I can't help you on that. I have my orders."

"Damn your orders. We've known each other for years. We've worked together, got drunk together..."

"Bumped uglies together?"

"That too," I added reluctantly.

"Don't worry. I can't officially help you. But I'm not going to leave a friend out on a limb. I might be able to point you in the right direction. There is nothing stopping me doing that."

I sighed in relief. This was progress.

"All you need is a passport and I know a guy who does the best passports in Croatia. In all of this part of Europe, in fact. And the good news is that he is based right here in Dubrovnik."

I was finally catching a break.

"How much?"

"It's not that simple. You don't have money and he, like everyone else, has been told not to help you. But there are ways. You need some leverage, something to convince him that it would be a good idea to help you out."

"Any suggestions? Maybe he will just fall for my boyish charms."

"Cherie, he doesn't swing that way," she said gently. "Not all of us are bowled over by your smile. But Milosz does have his weaknesses. And when a man is vulnerable he can be persuaded."

I looked off into the distance. I thought for a few minutes. I could wait for Bill to ride to my rescue and a few hours ago that would have seemed like an attractive proposition. But now I knew my location was compromised and I could be killed at any time. Without a gun I was vulnerable. So La Donna was my only hope. I looked all around me. This part of the street was deserted. I could see no dangers any place.

"So tell me about Milosz," I finally whispered.

"He is the best forger in the business," she said proudly, as if he was one of her protégées. "His parents were Poles who ended up in East Germany after the war. He grew up there and went to art college in Dresden. But his talent was never for creating his own works. He was a master mimic. He could do any style, and his precision... Of course, he came to the attention of the Stasi."

The East German secret police were one of the most feared security services on the planet, more ruthlessly efficient than the KGB ever were. If he was one of theirs he would be highly trained and very difficult to persuade. Those guys were hard men, even among us hard men. That might make my job more difficult. She went on with her story.

"He moved to Yugoslavia in the seventies, where he set up a printing business, here in Dubrovnik. It was a sort of semi-defection, escaping some trouble back home. At least, that was his cover story. But the truth was he was the Stasi's man over here and the print business was a cover. He worked for the East Germans and the Soviets right up to the fall of the Iron Curtain. And by the end the main job he did was provide the best false papers in Europe. Once the curtain fell he embraced free enterprise. Now his print works is the largest in Dubrovnik and he still does the other work. Only now he does it for the warlords, the criminal gangs, the human traffickers. They say that every passport he produces is a work of art, and he certainly charges the sort of prices only masterpieces can command."

"So your plan is that I rob a bank or pick a pocket or two to afford this guy's exorbitant prices?" I asked sarcastically.

"No, silly. You need your leverage. I am coming to that." She punched me playfully. "Really, you need to learn some patience."

So I sat and listened. I fell back on my mindfulness training. Focus on the breath coming in and out, focus on the feel of my body on the bench, focus on the sounds coming and going on the soft evening air, focus on not snapping at her to get on with it.

"Milosz has two weaknesses. He loves beautiful women and he loves his granddaughter. But not in that way. He is not a pervert."

I nodded my understanding.

"He loves not just beautiful women, but all women. He has what you call the ... the roving eye?"

I nodded again.

"Roving eye – funny expression. He also has the roving hands. He chases anything in a skirt."

"I left my kilt at home," I said.

"Silly boy – shut up and listen. His wife, she does not like this roving eye business. She is very pissed off at Milosz and a few weeks ago she threw him out of the house. So now he is living in a small room at the back of the print works with just two men to protect him. So that is where he is vulnerable. Attack at night, overcome his bodyguards, and you have him."

I grinned. "I can do that."

She shook her head.

"If only it were that easy. He has been trained by the Stasi. He is not going to make you a passport unless he wants to make you one. You can hold a gun to his head, break his legs, he still won't do what you want. That is the way they were trained. By the time you have broken him, there won't be enough of him left to do the document. So, you need leverage. That's where his other weakness comes in."

"Drink?"

"Shut up and listen. I already said – he loves his granddaughter. Paulina is seventeen and the apple of his eye. Already one eager boyfriend has been kneecapped. He is very protective. So here is what you do..."

Her plan was bold. It was also nasty and vicious. Pure La Donna. But it was clever. I could see it working. I went through it from all angles and I couldn't find the flaw.

"When?" I asked.

117

NINETEEN

At eight-thirty I left the hotel through the kitchen and out the rear exit. I had my phone and my wallet and a couple of other things I thought I might need. All that was missing was a weapon. And a bullet-proof vest. That last would have been a great comfort to me but, in its absence, I substituted caution. I stayed in the shadows, scanning the streets ahead and behind me. I couldn't see any danger but I hadn't seen any danger before I was shot at earlier either, so that signified nothing. At this rate it would take me all night to make it to the house in the suburbs where Paulina lived. I would need a disguise. Luckily I had an idea.

There was a church about two hundred metres from the hotel, an old one with ancient sandstone walls and a beautiful spire dominating the skyline. It wasn't the oldest or most venerable church in the town, but one was as good as another for my purposes. It took me ten minutes to cover the distance and as I approached the side door I was fairly sure I had not been seen. Shadows were lengthening across the square and the door was in deep shade. I slipped in quietly and briefly allowed my eyes to adjust to the darkness. There were two elderly women near the front of the church, kneeling, and to one side a man – clearly a tourist – was examining an ornate panel that seemed to be a scene of Jesus carrying the cross. But from my distance, and in the dim light, it could just as easily have been Jesus playing strip poker. Whatever, he was too engrossed to notice my entrance. So I slipped to the back of the church and knelt at a pew, my hands in front of me as if in prayer.

After a few minutes the man moved to another panel, then walked out the door I had come in. Not long after a stooped figure emerged from a door to the side of the altar and whispered briefly to the two women. Then he scanned the body of the church and saw me at the back. He called something across the space and I raised a hand in acknowledgement. The church was closing in a few minutes. I hadn't got that from what he had shouted. I had seen the closing time on the door on my way in.

The two women stood and began walking towards the back of the church. As they reached the centre of the church they turned and made a brief bow towards the altar. I took that moment to stand and slip into the shadows beside a large statue of one of the saints. I don't know which one, but you might. He was the one in the brown robes with the bald head. Come to think of it, that's most of them.

The two women walked to the end of the church and paused near the main door, where they lit a candle. They opened the door, allowing a crack of light to travel across the nave towards the altar. Then they were gone, the door closed and the light vanished.

I moved again, slipping into one of the confession boxes that dotted the side of the church. There were four on each side, each one big enough to hold the priest and the kneeling penitent. The wooden structures were completely private. I sat on the priest's narrow bench and waited. A few minutes later the stooped man reappeared. I could see him clearly through the grill of the confessional, but I knew I was virtually invisible inside unless he decided to check each one before closing. And no one is that meticulous.

Sure enough, after a quick walk around the church, he pulled the rear door closed and bolted it, then went to the side door and did the same. He crossed the church to the altar, where he briefly knelt on one knee and blessed himself. Then he walked through the door at the side of the altar and disappeared. I waited ten minutes and gave it another five just to be sure. Then I opened the confessional and crossed to the altar. I didn't bother with the genuflection. I walked straight up to the side door and put my ear to the ancient wood. Nothing. Not a sound. So I pushed through and found myself in the sacristy, the inner sanctum of the church. This was the backstage area where the priests prepared for their services. What I needed would be there.

The room was as black as the pit of hell. There was no light at all because there were no windows. I found the flashlight app on my phone and scanned it around the space, revealing a narrow room that ran the full length of the altar, but only about three metres wide. All along the wall opposite me was a long counter of rich amber wood, with presses underneath. Both side walls contained tall cupboards. I would need light to search this room properly. It was probably safe to switch on the electric light, but you never know. There might be a small sliver of a window high up, or light could escape under a door. So I rejected that idea. Instead, I searched the drawers until I found a box of candles, many half burned. I took out three and lit them, casting an eerie glow in the long narrow space. Then I threw open the first cupboard. Nothing but long staffs, oversized crucifixes, statues and other processional paraphernalia. So I went to the other side and opened one of the cupboards there. Bingo.

It was full of robes. I brought over the three candles and set them on the ground, throwing as much light as possible on the collection. What I was looking for were the long black cassocks that priests wear when they are not at the altar. I knew that if I threw on those dark robes, which reach to the ankle, I could walk around Dubrovnik and be completely invisible, just another clergyman going about his business. It took me less than a minute to discover, and another three to confirm, that there were no cassocks in the cupboard or in the neighbouring cupboard. There were all sorts of other vestments, but no cassocks. I was puzzled but then I recalled. Croatia, unlike the neighbouring countries, was Catholic. Cassocks are worn by Orthodox clergymen. Catholic priests wear a black suit, black shirt and white collar. And who keeps their suit in the church? They keep it in their home, ready to throw on in the morning.

This was a setback, but I wasn't leaving without a disguise. So I searched, eventually finding a white alb that went from neck down to knee. There was a mirror and in the dim light I looked at my reflection. Good, but something was missing. As it stood, I looked like a member of the Klu Klux Klan who had forgotten his pillow case. I went back to the cupboard and found a purple stole, the silk scarf that priests drape around the neck and let fall to their waist. The stole had an embroidered cross in yellow on both ends and completed the look. This would pass muster unless someone thought to ask themselves what a priest was doing in altar clothes walking the streets at night. But who gives priests a second glance anymore? I would get away with it.

The three candles went back in the drawer and I left the sacristy as I had found it, with no evidence of my nocturnal visit. I felt a twinge of guilt at stealing the robes and thought for a moment of dropping a few notes into one of the collection boxes in the church. But in the end I didn't feel that guilty and I kept my money.

I went to the side door of the church and tried the lock. Doors are an odd thing; most are only secure from one side. From the outside they are impregnable. From the inside you simply turn the knob and they open. But this was an old door and an old lock and it was firmly bolted. So even though I had broken into the church with no difficulty, I ended up having to pick the lock to break out.

TWENTY

I felt a bit self-conscious in my priestly robes and noticed as I walked down the busy streets near the town centre that drunks seemed to straighten up as I passed and couples on romantic walks still held hands but left a little gap between them, space for the holy spirit. I nodded at a few people, but quickly realised this was not needed or expected. So I kept my head high and walked as if I owned the streets.

I passed out of the centre quickly and once I was in the residential part of town I met fewer and fewer people. My progress was swift. It was not long after ten when I reached the address La Donna had given me. It was a quiet and affluent street, and the houses were all detached, with their own gardens. Whoever lived on this street was doing well. It smelt of money and was completely deserted.

Still, I took precautions. I walked past the house without a glance. Peripheral vision showed me everything I needed to know. No lights on at the front, but some light spilling out around the side, meaning there was a window or more light up at the rear of the house. A small gate, a low fence and a few bushes in the garden. Not much cover, but a little. I walked on.

At the end of the street I turned a corner and found myself walking alongside a high wall. Trees lined the edge of the pavement. I paused and looked around. Like the other street, it was completely deserted so I took a moment to remove the bright white alb and the stole, bundling them up and putting them under my arm. White stands out in the dark like a target painted on your back. I turned and walked back towards the house.

All my senses were on alert. I heard nothing. I saw nothing. I felt nothing. I scanned the windows of nearby houses. No one was looking out. As I reached Paulina's house I placed one hand on the wall and quickly vaulted over, dropping on the ground on the other side. There was a crunch of gravel but no other sound. In the silence the crunch sounded like a jet taking off, but as I lay there no lights came on. I had not been spotted. So I stood cautiously and stowed the clerical robes between one of the bushes and the wall. Then I walked quickly to the house and slipped around the side. There were no lights on in the front and no sound of television or music, so it was safe to assume that half of the house was safe. I had to know about the back.

I turned the corner carefully. Light spilled out of a big window into the small garden. Light, but no sound. So I approached cautiously and peered in quickly. I was looking at the kitchen, and it was empty. I examined it more carefully. Nothing but a modern kitchen and a door leading out of it. I tried the back door. It was closed. It was locked. So I opened it. It took a matter of moments with my picking tools. I slipped inside and pulled the door closed behind me, gently, barely making a click.

The house felt empty. But you don't stay alive by trusting feelings. You check. I listened at the door of the kitchen for a full five minutes before pushing the handle and stepping through to the hallway. The door to the front room was open and I looked inside. It was the family room, with a sofa, two comfortable armchairs, a coffee table stacked with fashion magazines and a television in the corner. No occupants.

The other rooms downstairs were a small bedroom and a toilet, both empty. So I went upstairs, carefully walking on the edges of the steps rather than the centre to minimise creaks. I paused at the top. No sound. So I checked the rooms. The master bedroom was empty. So was the bathroom. So was the second bedroom, which was clearly Paulina's. It does not take a detective to figure out which room belongs to a teenage girl. The boy-band posters are a giveaway. I recognised Justin Bieber and didn't recognise a black rap artist. I am sure he was a rap artist; he was wearing a baseball cap jauntily backwards.

In one sense things were going well. I had broken into the target's house easily and without detection. In another sense they were not going well at all. In an ideal world I would have broken in, found my target asleep, done the job I had come to do and been on my way. Now I would have to wait. And I didn't know for how long.

I made myself as comfortable as I could. I crawled under the bed and stretched out, my body shoved against the wall. I made sure my feet did not stick out and give me away. My nose was only an inch or two away from below the mattress and I felt an almost irresistible urge to sneeze. Did she ever vacuum under here?

Snipers are trained to wait patiently, often lying for hours or days without movement, silently peeing into their pants without rustling the surrounding grass. They are masters of disappearing into the environment, ready to pop out with lethal force when the time comes. I am no sniper. I was bored, restless and beginning to cramp. I was also less than happy about the occasional spider that chose to run across my face. I don't know how long I remained there under that bed. I think about three weeks. I am fairly sure that is accurate, though the evidence of my watch later on would suggest it was a little under an hour. The watch must have stopped at some point during the evening.

I think I was in a daydream when the front door crashed open, because for a moment I forgot completely where I was and I tried to sit up. The mattress smashing against my nose stopped that and the resulting cloud of dust almost brought on a sneezing fit. For a few precious moments I struggled to bring the sneeze reflex under control. During those moments I heard and felt the front door slam shut and heard loud footsteps marching down the hallway into the kitchen. Then I heard the click of a kettle being turned on. For the next few minutes I interpreted the sounds as a sandwich being made. From here I could not tell what sort of sandwich, but the sounds reminded me that I was beginning to get hungry. Perhaps I should have had a dessert after my dinner with La Donna.

The footsteps marched back into the hallway and into the front room. I know it was the front room because suddenly the television came on, far too loud. I had to decide what to do. Was this Paulina downstairs? If so, I should creep down and get it over with. Or was it one of her parents? In which case creeping down prematurely was the last thing I wanted to do. I fingered the little something La Donna had given me for this portion of the plan. Get up or stay put?

The television flicked through several channels before setting on some horrible Euro-pop music station. I listened for a few minutes as it blared through the house. Had she no consideration for the neighbours?. If that was her parents' selection, the world was a sick place. Teenage girls, on the other hand, are not known for their taste. It was time to move.

TWENTY-ONE

The funny thing about being a man of action is that it takes so long. Time to move? I waited at the top of the stairs for a full five minutes to make sure that she settled and wasn't suddenly about to go to the kitchen for another sandwich. Then I snuck down the stairs and waited for another few moments, listening, outside the door.

She hadn't slammed it. It was half open, but opened inward, so it concealed some of the room. I could see the television screen flickering and she hadn't bothered to switch on a light. The noise from the television made listening a bit of a redundant exercise and the angle of the door made casing the room impossible. So I was standing there, putting off the inevitable. And the longer I stood the more likely it was that the parents would come home, which would really screw my plans. I reached into my pocket and took out the one bit of help La Donna had given me. No weapon, but a tiny aerosol spray, the type people use to spray scented water on their faces during hot spells. It was a small plastic container that fitted neatly into my fist with a tiny nozzle on the end. I don't know exactly what it was filled with, but some form of chloroform or ether was my guess. One spray, she had said, and the girl would pass out and remain firmly unconscious for at least five minutes.

Of course the plan had been to sneak up on her in her

bedroom in the deep of night and spray her without alerting her. The problem with spraying strange substances into the faces of victims is that many victims show a terrible reluctance to breath in those miasmic mists. It would be easier if she didn't see it coming. But there was no help for it.

I tried to figure out reflections from the television screen, which was difficult with the kaleidoscope of images the pop videos were throwing up. But between songs the screen went dark for a fleeting second and I could see enough to tell me my target was on one of the two armchairs. She might be asleep, or she might be reclining after a difficult day being a moody teen.

I stepped through the door.

She was slumped, her legs stretched out straight, her back rounded, her head staring at the screen, eyes closed. She was a good-looking girl of about seventeen, with long dark hair but a pout on her face that suggested she gave her parents ulcers. On her lap was a plate with an uneaten sandwich, and balanced precariously on the arm of the chair was a full mug of coffee. I had caught a break; she was asleep. But I was taking no chances. I sprayed the mist directly into her face. She stirred slightly, then sighed and seemed to settle even more into the comfortable chair. I sprayed her twice more to make sure. I put the coffee mug on the floor where it would not spill and removed the sandwich plate. I was tempted to take a bite but there was coleslaw in it. Who ruins a sandwich with coleslaw?

There was one final bit to do. I went into the kitchen and opened the cutlery drawer, removing the sharpest and most vicious carving knife I could find. Then I returned to Paulina. I was ready.

I pulled her up in the armchair and pushed her head back, exposing the pale flesh of her neck. I stood behind her and rested her head against my right shoulder. Then I placed the edge of the knife against the side of her neck and pressed down into the flesh. Not enough to draw blood, but enough to make my intent clear. With my left hand I took out my phone and angled it above my head. When I was sure it was just perfect, I took the photo.

I was delighted with the result. My face was not visible, just one brawny arm and the vicious knife. It looked like a still from a horror flick; the helpless girl with her head thrown back, her face blank like she was stoned. The flash had bled the colour from her, which helped make her look more pathetic and vulnerable. This was the photo that would give any loving grandfather nightmares. It was the photo that would get me a passport. La Donna's plan was coming together.

I texted the photo to La Donna, then put the phone back in my pocket. I pulled the girl by the ankles until she was slumped once more before the television, then replaced the coffee mug on the arm of her chair. I put the plate and sandwich back on her lap. There might be time for me to go to the kitchen and make one for myself, without the coleslaw.

I took one final look around the room and was about to walk out when the front door banged open.

TWENTY-TWO

I had about two seconds, so no great thought went into my next move. I dived behind the sofa and scrunched up in the space between it and the wall. I was back among the dust and the spiders. And now I absolutely positively had to control the sneeze reflex.

It was dark behind the sofa because Paulina had not switched on the lights when she sat down to enjoy her sandwich. But it didn't remain dark for long. Two sets of footsteps – and two giggling bodies with them – came into the room and the light blazed on. I could make out a female giggle and a deeper male growling laugh. Obviously the parents were home. And they weren't happy to find their daughter slumped in front of a television and out like a light.

The deep growling laugh of the father turned to a more guttural tone as he began shouting at his daughter. I couldn't see what was happening but it didn't take a genius to work it out. He was pissed off. Then the mother began shouting. Obviously she was pissed off too. Then I heard the chair move and knew they were shaking her. She was deeply asleep. At least I knew the stuff La Donna had given me had worked. But perhaps I should have left it at one squirt.

Finally the teenager responded. I heard the petulant snarl. There were three raised voices for a few minutes, then a lull, then the coffee mug fell over and the voices rose in an ugly cacophony. The girl picked up her plate and walked towards the kitchen. It is amazing how much you can follow just from voices and footsteps. I heard heavy footsteps going up the stairs. The daughter was off to bed. That only left the parents. As soon as they retired, I would slip out. To hell with my sandwich, I would go hungry.

But the sofa creaked heavily as the father flopped down on it. He lowered the sound of the television and began surfing the channels. There was some soft conversation, then the wife left the room and I heard the kettle going on once more in the kitchen. More than five minutes passed before she returned. From the clinks as she sat I guessed she had brought tea or coffee for both of them. She sat down beside him and the sofa creaked again. From the creak, she wasn't a petite woman.

There was quietness for a while. The husband had settled on a football game – I could see the reflection of the TV screen bounced off a small photo frame on the far wall. I don't think it was a great game. But I am not a football fan and my viewing conditions were hardly ideal. His wife was snuggled against him. That I couldn't see in the reflections. It was supposition on my part, based on the fact that the sofa had bulged dangerously against me on one end, but not on the other, meaning they were sitting side by side. Football games last ninety minutes so potentially I was stuck there for that long. But I didn't think they would watch it to the end. Especially if the wife was cosying up to the husband. They would take the action upstairs and I could make my escape.

After about ten minutes their mugs were placed on the floor

and a minute later I heard soft romantic whispers. Then there
was a sharp intake of breath and she said something to him.
But she wasn't annoyed because she laughed as she said it. The
soft whisperings became more urgent and the sofa began to
rock. They weren't taking it upstairs.

I had to lie there with spiders running across me, dust motes
dancing above my delicate nostrils, while the two got very busy.
As they had a teenage daughter they must have been married
a number of years, but they still seem unable to keep their
hands off each other. The movements became more frantic
and chaotic and suddenly something came over the edge of
the sofa, landing across my face. I almost cried out. Whatever
it was, its loss hadn't thrown them off their stride. When it
became obvious that no hand would come looking for it, I
stretched up to my face and felt with my fingers. Stiff fabric
in a circular shape ... wire ... damn, her bra had landed on my
face.

The perfect end to a perfect night.

I lay there and thought of my mindfulness then decided to
hell with that. There was no mindfulness that would make
this any better. So I lay there and fumed. It lasted twenty
minutes, a tribute to their stamina. Then the husband began
snoring. But the wife was breathing softly. It was not the
pattern of someone sleeping. She was lying there beside him
contemplating life, or washing, or whatever it is women think
about when their menfolk fall asleep once their animal needs
are satisfied. And as long as she remained awake I remained
trapped. So I lay there.

It took fifteen minutes, and my ordeal was ended quite suddenly. There was a movement above me and the husband fell off the sofa, waking up with a curse. He muttered something and left the room, his footsteps echoing up the stairs. A minute later she followed. I was alone.

I gave it ten minutes, spiders or no spiders. Then I got up, tossed aside the bra and walked to the kitchen. I let myself out the back door without stopping at the fridge, collected the cassock from behind the bush and hurried back to the hotel.

When I got back the bar was still open, but only the stragglers were left. I took no chances. I went around the rear and entered the hotel that way, slipping quietly upstairs. La Donna was in bed asleep. She barely stirred when I crept in and I didn't switch on the light. I took off my shoes and trousers and looked at the chair. Then I looked at the bed. It had been a long night. I pulled back the covers and got in beside her.

She stirred briefly and put an arm across my chest. She was still asleep but it was a light sleep and her hand began to slip down my chest. I clutched the aerosol and sprayed it softly in her face once, twice, then a third time to be sure. I rolled over and went to sleep.

TWENTY-THREE

It was the smell of coffee that woke me in the morning. It was a pungent and rich aroma and I woke with a smile. The sunlight was streaming through the window and La Donna was sitting in the bed beside me, looking very alluring in black silk. But the breakfast was even more alluring. There were fresh croissants, two boiled eggs and crusty bread with feta cheese and slices of large ripe tomatoes. And freshly squeezed orange juice.

"This makes a nice change from yesterday," I said.

"I am sorry, Cherie. I had to leave in a hurry yesterday. Today I can linger and enjoy breakfast with you. You were magnificent last night." She ran a finger down my chest, sending electric tingles through my skin.

"You were asleep last night and even if you hadn't been, you got quite enough use out of my body the night before."

I spread the feta on the bread and topped it with a slice of tomato. It was as delicious as it had looked. I took a sip of coffee. The world began to look better.

"The picture you took was great. That will do the trick."

Her words brought me back with a crash. Last night had been a horrible few hours, but a successful few hours. I just had to stay alive another twelve then use my leverage on Paulina's grandfather and this nightmare would come to an end.

"Can you get me a gun?" I asked.

"Bold," she replied. "You know the rules. I can't help you. Isn't it enough that I am letting you use my body and my bed?"

I let that one go.

La Donna left around ten o'clock and this time I didn't have to waste my time on silly handcuffs and restraints. All I had to do was pull back the covers and step out of the bed. Which I did. It had been pleasant to sit there watching her dress. A gentleman would have turned away, but a gentleman would have missed a great show because she had taken her time, lingering over each item.

I needed a quick, cold, shower. Then I got dressed.

It took me nearly an hour to reach the café where I had met Jelly the previous day. Not surprisingly she wasn't there. We had made no arrangements and when we had parted the previous afternoon I had known it was forever. But I felt strangely disappointed. Still, I had a day to kill and one café was as good as another. I went in and ordered a cappuccino and a croissant and picked a table near the rear where I could see the entire street and every table in the café. No one was going to sneak up on me today.

The coffee arrived and I sipped. Perfect. I got out my phone and tried Bill. He answered at the first ring.

"Hello, you are through to the lingerie department. How can I help you today?"

"I had a bra I could have donated to your department last night but I don't have it any more. Long story," I said.

"I have all day," he replied. "Nothing but blue skies and blue sea for miles and miles and miles around me. What the fuck do people see in sailing? It's the most boring way to spend a vacation."

"You arrived safely?"

"Yes and no," he said. "We got here all right and the army provided a helicopter for the flight down south to get the boat. Everything went smoothly. And my son is a natural at this. Without him I'd be drifting towards Libya right now. But I couldn't get a gun."

I knew the feeling. Without a gun Bill would feel naked.

"You have contacts."

"Sure. But I'm on vacation. If I ask for a gun my people will ask why. Then my leave will be cancelled and you'll be screwed. Talking of being screwed, how's La Donna."

"She seems to be on side but taking her own sweet time about it. The word is out that no one is to help me and they are actively hunting me. A sniper nearly got me yesterday afternoon."

"Shit."

"But I think I can get papers tonight off an old Stasi guy. Ever hear of Milosz Vogt?"

"Yeah," said Bill. "The bastard's dead."

That shook me.

"Are you sure?"

"Sure? What's sure in this business? He tried to leave East Germany long time ago and was never heard of since. Why do you ask?"

"La Donna says he's here, still churning out the best

passports in Europe. She said he was a double for the Stasi and never left them."

There was a silence on the phone, then Bill said: "Makes sense. If you can get a Vogt passport you can go anywhere in the world. And if you can confirm he is still alive I will have some interesting intel to deliver back to Langley after this vacation. In fact, I'll be able to chalk it down to work and get those vacation days back. Win win. Do you think you can make it out?"

"I should be able to. But don't cancel plan B. When will you arrive in Dubrovnik?"

"Mid-afternoon tomorrow," he said.

I ordered a second coffee and a second croissant, after lingering as long as possible on the first. I killed another hour. The place was beginning to fill up with lunchtime customers. I was a dead table. I knew that soon enough a waiter would come over and politely suggest I finish up and move on. So I stood, leaving a few notes on the table to cover the bill. Maybe I could spend a few hours snoozing in the confessional of the church I had hidden in last night.

I turned towards the door. And saw her.

TWENTY-FOUR

She had walked in unnoticed while I was looking for change for my coffees and was in the centre of the room, looking around slowly, a slightly wistful look on her face. Then she saw me and the wistful look changed into a bright smile.

Jelly was wearing tight jeans that showed off her shapely legs to perfection and a short-sleeved white blouse. A white baseball cap hid most of her dark hair and she looked gorgeous.

"You look good enough to eat," I said.

"Then I hope you are hungry," she smiled as she sat.

"I was just leaving," I said.

"Don't you have a few minutes to buy a girl some lunch?"

I sat again. "Not only do I have a few minutes, today I even have a wallet and a respectable set of clothes."

She cast an appraising eye over me and said: "Not bad. Did you steal the clothes of a more trendy man this morning?"

"No. My clothes were returned last night."

As soon as I said it I knew it was a mistake. I didn't want to tell her too much. It wasn't that I didn't trust her, but at the moment I was toxic. Any involvement with me could be dangerous and I didn't want to put her in that danger. A quick lunch and I would disappear.

"It's a long story," I ended lamely.

"Fine. Don't tell me. Let's get a table outside, in the sun."

"I have a headache. I need the shade."

We ordered our food. She went for a salad, I got a plate of calamari. We ordered two glasses of white wine. But something was missing. The easiness of the previous day was gone. I am not a man with a great deal of emotional intelligence but even I could tell there was a problem. Finally she tackled it head on.

"You know I worked in the military police for years? I've investigated all sorts of things, from pilfered supplies to guys selling secrets wholesale to the enemy. In all the investigations there has been one common thread. Guys lying to me. It gets so that you have a sort of sixth sense about it, a built-in bullshit detector. And mine is pinging right now."

She looked at me. I said nothing. So she went on: "You said your clothes has been stolen, yet here you are in your own clothes. Items don't get returned like that, not wallets anyway. You might find some of your clothes scattered by the thieves, but not your wallet. And who steals clothes anyway? Ping, ping. The bullshit detector is going off. As I see it, you have two options; you can level with me or I can finish my salad and walk away and never see your lying face again."

"That's a bit severe," I protested.

"That's life as a woman, Eli. Men lie to us all the time. You think you find a good one, one who is a bit different from the others. Turns out he is just a different kind of liar."

I leaned back and scanned the room. I looked into her face, seeing some hurt but more steely determination. And I made up my mind.

"Okay, I may have lied a little to you. But my only reason

is that I didn't want to involve you in my problems. I had no other motive."

"Let me be the judge of that."

I sipped my wine thoughtfully. Where to start and how much to tell?

"Did you ever serve in Northern Ireland?"

She shook her head.

"You knew people who did, at any rate. It was one of the toughest postings, but the worst of it was before our time. I've spoken to vets about it and I am sure you have too. The regular soldiers were targets and spent most of their time in barracks or on patrol. No mixing with the community. But there were other soldiers, the shadow men. They didn't go out in big patrols. They stayed on their own. And they didn't wear uniforms on a lot of their missions. The hard men, the undercover guys."

She nodded: "The Special Reconnaissance Unit and their successors. Some would say that's not proper soldiering."

"And some would say that you fight fire with fire."

"That's stupid. You fight fire with water."

My attempt at an explanation was not going as well as I had hoped.

"You weren't old enough to serve in the Special Reconnaissance Unit anyway," she said, as if that put an end to the matter.

"I was never in the army," I snapped. "I came to this work through other avenues."

"What work?" she asked, not an unreasonable question.

"I am not a spy," I replied. "But sometimes my legitimate work brings me to interesting places. And I have been known to dig out information or pass on messages for our government and other friendly interests. Small jobs they couldn't do themselves without a diplomatic incident. That's why I was in Mostar. Tying up loose ends from the trouble in the nineties. Only someone double-crossed me and of course the government need deniability, so I am on my own."

I was glad to see her military training kicking in. She didn't ask for details. Instead she stretched across the table and held my hand.

"Is there anything I can do?"

"I'm afraid not. A colleague of mine is helping me get false papers to get me home. She's the one who stole my clothes, because she felt I would be safer remaining holed up rather than walking the streets here."

"That's a bit paranoid."

"My thoughts exactly. So I went out yesterday. And not long after I left you a sniper took a shot at me. He came very close to killing me."

Her face went pale.

"But you should be hiding."

"I'm in the shade here, out of sight of the street."

She hit me on the arm, hard.

"That's not what I meant. We need to get you somewhere safe."

"There is no 'we'. I need to stay safe for another few hours, until I have my papers. You need to keep away from me so that you don't get caught in the crossfire."

"I can help."

"You were military police, not special forces. And now you're a teacher. I have a range of skills that will probably keep me alive until I get out of here. And this restaurant is clean. I have been here all morning. So relax, enjoy your salad and leave the worrying to people above your pay grade and mine."

She didn't seem convinced but deep down she must have known there was little she could do to help me and that her presence could complicate things. So, after a brief internal struggle, her face returned to the wide smile I was beginning to like a lot and she began to talk about her plans for when her brother would finally make Europe. And to further the distraction, I told her about my sister, the porn star.

We had a very pleasant lunch, at the end of which she slipped me the address of her hotel and made me promise I would contact her in the morning if there was any difficulty with my new papers. I made the promise and stood to let her leave. She looked into my eyes uncertainly then took the plunge, reaching forward and holding my face in her hands. We kissed. It began tentatively but soon there was nothing tentative about it. My tongue got a better workout than if I had tried to learn Finnish and the softness of her body against mine filled me with yearning. There was so much promise in that kiss. But in the end, I had to let her go.

TWENTY-FIVE

La Donna made me wait.

I was back in the hotel room a full two hours, stretched out on the bed staring at the ceiling, before she arrived. What I wouldn't do for a good book. Mindfulness is fine but it doesn't kill two hours.

She flounced into the room and sat on the bed, locking her lips on mine in a passionate kiss. We were colleagues but there was nothing collegial in her lips or in her hands as they roved up and down my body. I just thought of Jelly and played along. Luckily La Donna had nothing serious on her mind. She was simply being a tease because that was her default mode when dealing with men. Soon she released me and I sat up.

"Are you ready?" she asked.

"Let's go over the geography one more time."

She sighed.

"Okay, he lives in the rear of his print works. The print works is located in an industrial estate in the new harbour, about an hour from here on foot. There are three premises on the block, his being the middle one. The other two will be closed at night. You get in, overcome his two guards, and secure him. Then you text me and I text you the photo of his granddaughter. Once he sees her he will do what you want. It takes four hours for him to do a passport and you need to be away by six tomorrow morning. So that is your window. Do everything right, you have a passport, you get on a plane, you fly home. Get it wrong and you are on your own."

"I need a gun."

"I cannot give you a gun."

"There are two guards and he might be armed himself. What am I meant to do, punch them out?"

"Improvise. Find something you can use as a weapon."

"And where would you suggest I look for something like that?"

"I don't know – you could start with the drawers in this room."

There was something in the way she said it. So I looked. I opened the bedside locker and saw nothing. So I went to the chest of drawers and opened one of the two top drawers. Her underwear. She laughed. I opened the second drawer. Nestling there on a folded pair of jeans was a small pistol. I picked it up. It was tiny, what used to be called a lady's gun. It would fit comfortably in a handbag or purse without weighing it down or leaving a bulge. It would fit in a suit pocket the same way.

I held it and despite its tiny size it felt snug in my hands, like it belonged to me. I raised my hand and sighted down the barrel. It would do.

"I thought you couldn't..."

"I can't give you a gun. That was made clear to me. But if you find a gun someone carelessly abandoned, I don't have to take it from you. Congratulations. You have found a gun someone carelessly abandoned."

The gun was a Baby Browning. Designed between the wars,

it held just six rounds and weighed ten ounces fully loaded. The rounds were low velocity and didn't carry much punch, but put one in a guy's leg and he wasn't going to chase you. Put it between his eyes and he would never chase anyone again. I wasn't a sniper. Any shooting I would do this night would be up close and personal. This gun would do as well as another. I slipped out the magazine and checked. It was fully loaded.

"Do you have a spare magazine?"

"No – that's all you get. And if you use it you will be bringing heat down on me, so I would be very happy if it comes back with all six rounds still there."

"I'll do my best," I promised. I was no fan of collateral damage anyway.

The rest of the gear La Donna had assembled for me. There was a flashlight, some basic lock-picking tools, a glass tumbler and a roll of black duct tape. We were good to go but there were a few hours left to kill, so we ordered dinner. I was eating a lot out here; but hopefully the night's exercise would work it all off.

At nine I left the hotel by the rear and took about ten minutes to make my first hundred metres, heading in the wrong direction. But when I was sure no one was following me, I doubled back and walked through the darkening streets towards the harbour. Along the way I went through the plan and my preparations. As usual I had forgotten something. I had a gun but I should have stolen a knife from the hotel. Too late now. As I passed a roadside café I slipped a fork from a table and put it in my pocket. It was the first thing to come to hand. A few minutes later I found a quiet alley and disappeared down it, where I taped the fork to my ankle with the duct tape. Even the pros often overlook the ankle when carrying out a body search.

I got to the industrial estate at ten minutes before ten, a bit quicker than La Donna had predicted. A busy road forked, one way leading into the harbour and industrial estate, the other heading off along the coast road. Cars and trucks whizzed by and there were plenty of people about. It felt safe. Any serious attempt on my life would wait until I was a bit more isolated. So I relaxed and made good progress. I took the road leading to the harbour and passed the harbour entrance, marked by two large pillars with nothing between them. In my head I had a map. Now was the chance to see how accurate that map had been.

The industrial estate was separated from the harbour by the road. The estate was made up of several blocks, each containing a number of businesses. At the front were three blocks. According to La Donna, the print works was the middle premises of the third block, furthest away from the harbour entrance. I could see it ahead of me. Behind the row of three blocks were two other rows, meaning nine blocks and perhaps thirty businesses in the estate.

The harbour road was not busy. It led nowhere so there was no passing traffic, only vehicles that had business going in and out of the area. The absence of passing cars would make my job so much easier. The harbour itself contained a mix of boats, from small commercial fishing vessels, tugs and dredges right up. Some had lights on and showed signs of activity. Others did not.

The one thing La Donna had not warned me about was what dominated the entire landscape. A cruise ship that must have been two hundred and fifty metres long was pulled right up to the harbour wall. Several storeys of apartments were lit up like Christmas and the passenger decks were thronged. And every person on board would have a clear view of me breaking into the print works.

TWENTY-SIX

When faced with adversity, according to my late father, you can curl up and cry or you can try to muddle through. I wanted to curl up and cry, but I didn't see how that would improve my situation. So I went for the other option. I decided to case the building as if there were no cruise ship. I strolled nonchalantly along the road as if I had no cares in the world. Skulking in the shadows would not work here; that was a sure way of drawing attention to myself.

I took my time so that I would have plenty of opportunity to scope out the printing works. It was exactly as La Donna had told me. First was a fish processing plant. This operated from six in the morning to eight in the evening and was already closed. Next was the print works itself. It occupied the middle of the block. At the front was a small door into the office area and a big sliding door that could take a van. This was where print jobs were collected. That door would open on to the print room floor. Both were closed. Presumably both were locked.

The end of the block was occupied by a large furniture retailer. They took a siesta in the afternoon and were open late most evenings, she had said. I could see this was true. The lights were on and there were plenty of customers milling around. I turned the corner and walked around the furniture outlet to the rear of the block. I did a complete loop. The rear of the print factory was a huge door, big enough to take large lorries. This was obviously for paper deliveries. There was no small door. Because I was out of view of the harbour I was able to take my time and examine the door. It was securely bolted. I could have opened it with the right equipment. But you don't pick a big lock with small tools. And if I had unlocked it, it would not have slid open quietly. So I could forget about the rear. It was thorough the front door or nothing.

I walked on, rounding the fish factory. The first workers would arrive shortly before six in the morning, but the furniture place would not open for three hours after that. So it was the fish workers I had to be concerned about. I would have to be finished in the print works by five-thirty. As it took four hours to do up a passport, I would have to have secured the guards and scared Milosz into cooperation by one-thirty at the latest. There was plenty of time.

I walked around to the front of the block and milled with the people coming and going near the cruise ship. It was huge, a floating city with all the character of an inner city high-rise. Several locals were looking up in awe and the crew seemed to accept this as their due. So I was able to walk right up and examine the gangplank without arousing the slightest suspicion. According to the sign printed in French, German and English, passengers would have to embark by eleven-thirty and the ship sailed at midnight.

This was a bit of a problem. Cruise ships normally arrive in a town in the morning and let their passengers disgorge for the day. But they leave in the early evening to get to their next port by the following day. It might have been engine trouble, tides, weather, but for some reason this boat was out of sync. On a normal day it would have already left Dubrovnik, but today I would have an audience until midnight. Which reduced my window of action considerably.

There was nothing for it. I ambled along the street and when no one was looking I slipped into the delivery yard of the fish factory. The place stank, but at least it was empty. I found a corner and curled up. I went to sleep for an hour.

I woke around twenty minutes past eleven and went back out on to the road. The furniture store was deserted and the sky was dark. But the area was still lit up like a football stadium for a night game. The bloody cruise liner. If that was not there I would already be carrying out my break-in, leaving myself a huge margin for errors.

I joined the crowd, which had thinned from earlier. Most of the locals had gone home. A steady trickle of people arrived from the town and walked the gangplank to the reception deck. Two officers in gaudy uniforms stood at the bottom to greet the guests and loud music came from a string quartet on board. I kept scanning the crowd. Most of them looked like they should; latecomers rushing to make the sailing, arrogant drunks not worried in the slightest about delaying their fellow passengers, crew members taking their last stroll on dry land. One guy seemed to be slightly out of place. He was too poorly dressed to be one of the passengers and was straying too far away from the ship to be crew. He looked at me twice in passing and then the penny dropped. He was security, probably for the industrial estate. They had a night-watchman.

I tried to time my walking so that I was as far away as possible from him. By eleven forty-five the trickle from town had dwindled to nothing. By five to twelve I was growing concerned; the gangplank still hadn't been pulled up. The two guys in the gaudy uniforms were getting restless. One of them took out a walkie-talkie and it hissed as he spoke to someone on board. After a few minutes he wrote down something – a number – and handed it to the other man, who took out a cellphone and made the call. It was in English and I was close enough to hear one end of it.

"We said in five minutes. You miss the ship. We all waiting for you. You the last." Pause. "No, not ten minutes. You get here now. We don't hold ten minutes. We hold five."

In the end they held for fifteen, and a very drunk man staggered to the gangplank. He was effusive in his apologies and tried to slip the two guys some notes, which they brusquely rejected. They almost pushed him up the gangplank, which was then mechanically raised. The last passenger was on board.

The string quartet had packed up quite a while ago, its music replaced by a blare from the on-board disco. Most of the lights were still on. I stood there, staring at the big ship, willing it to take off. I willed it so intently I forgot that I was standing there on my own, the only man in an otherwise deserted harbour. How could the security man miss me? A rookie mistake.

When I became aware of him approaching me I did the only

thing I could. I swayed slightly. I turned to him and smiled vacantly. I took a step towards the ship and slightly missed my footing, then straightened up immediately. There is a secret to playing a drunk; underplay it. Drunks retain a sort of natural dignity. They desperately try to walk in a straight line and not to fudge their words. If you ever need to play a convincing drunk, try to imagine you are a drunk trying to play sober. I looked at the night-watchman, waved blearily, then turned back to the ship and called out: "Mikhail — bon voyage."

I began to walk away, carefully, trying not to sway or stagger. I could hear no footsteps so he wasn't following me. But I knew he would continue to watch me. So I kept walking, down the full length of the ship then out the harbour entrance on to the main road. It was only at that point that I dared to turn around. He had turned away and resumed his rounds. So I turned and walked back into the harbour. Two hours late, it was finally on.

TWENTY-SEVEN

I was back in the industrial estate and at least now I didn't have to case the target building. I could get straight to work – once I knew the schedule of the night-watchman. I hid in the fish factory yard again and waited. Sure enough, twenty minutes later, he passed by at a leisurely pace. I watched him as he walked along the harbour road, then turned when he got to the end and disappeared into the industrial estate. Assuming that was his normal pace, I had more than twenty minutes before he came back. Plenty of time to carry out the break-in.

It was now fast approaching one o'clock and my time was running out.

I approached the print works carefully. I needed to avoid any possible security cameras. One of his men could be monitoring them. There might also be a motion sensor triggering a light. The last thing I needed was to let them know I was coming. So I hung to the side of the building. Most motion sensors are designed to catch something coming towards a building, not something clinging to the wall. I got to the door without incident.

I took out my flashlight and had a quick look at the lock. It was a Yale, wouldn't you know? Yales were sold initially as unpickable, but that's simply untrue. They can be picked. It just takes a few more minutes. I took out the glass tumbler and put it to the door, listening for a few minutes. I heard nothing, so

I put away the tumbler and got out my tools. I had a thin wire to jog the tumblers into position and a stiff piece of sprung steel as the tensioner. I carefully jiggled the first tumbler into position, applied the tension to hold it, jiggled the second, held it, jiggled the third, nothing. I jiggled it again. Nothing. Damn.

I released the tension on the first two tumblers and let them fall back. Something was sticking in the lock. A bit of oil would make a huge difference but I had none. So I blew gently into the keyhole then ran the wire through it aggressively once or twice to dislodge whatever dirt was hampering me. I tried it again.

The first and second tumbler came up and I held them. Then the third came up. I held it. If the other two yielded, I was in. They did. The lock gave with a soft click and I held the door open a quarter of an inch. Then I waited. After a minute I still heard nothing. So I pushed the door open and stepped into the small vestibule.

This was not what I expected. I was in a small sectioned-off area of corridor. There was a door in front of me that led into the main office area. And that door was protected by a keypad.

Here's the thing about keypads: there are a huge number of combinations you need to try to open them. If you do the maths, you have ten digits to choose from for the first number, nine for the second, eight for the third and seven for the fourth. That makes 5040 possible combinations. If you can go through ten combinations a minute – and I defy anyone to move their fingers that fast – you could be stuck there the bones of eight hours. And some have a feature that if you try unsuccessfully three times in a row the lock is immobilised for a minute or more. So make that eight hours two days, realistically.

Of course, some people leave the number scrawled on the wall to remind themselves. It defeats the purpose of a keypad but you would be surprised how often you get lucky. I ran the flashlight all over the wall. I wasn't getting lucky today.

I looked at the keypad and saw four numbers were polished clean by countless fingers rubbing against them, while six of the digits were caked with grime. The clean digits were 1, 4, 8 and 9. These were the numbers that were being pressed every day. So the combination I was looking for was made up of these four numbers. Now the maths became more favourable. I had four possibilities for the first number, three for the second, two for the third, and only one for the fourth. So instead of over five thousand possibilities I was looking at twenty-four. That was only a few minutes' work. I had caught a break.

I could have just started logically, going through every possibility. But often numbers have a meaning. People choose a code that they can remember because the numbers have significance for them. Birthday? Year he got married? I looked at the four polished digits and then it hit me. What if Milosz had been born in 1948? Made sense, according to the biography La Donna had given me. I had nothing to lose by trying it so keyed in the four numbers and heard the satisfying buzz as the lock electronically disengaged. I pushed the door open an inch and waited. I heard no sound. Not a peep. So

I pushed the door open fully and stepped through, closing it gently behind me.

I found myself in a small corridor with three offices leading off to my right. At the end of the corridor was a door leading to the print works itself. And all along the left wall were a series of windows that allowed a full view of the factory floor. I ducked down so that no one on the floor could see me in the corridor and took out my phone and angled it above my head, using the screen as a mirror. I scanned the whole floor and saw nothing suspicious. That didn't mean anything; it was hardly a forensic search of the premises. But I felt sure enough to stand again and approach the first door.

I held up the glass tumbler and listened for a minute. No sound. Holding my gun in my hand I pushed the door gently open and stepped into the receptionist's office. It was empty. I went to the second room and repeated the process; listen, open, enter, search. Nothing. The third office, the same. All three offices were completely empty, just like you would expect in premises that were closed for the night. La Donna had said that he had a bed in a room at the back of the plant. It looked as if her intelligence was good.

I came back into the corridor and as I did the silence was filled with the sound of a toilet flushing. I dropped to the floor like I had been shot.

TWENTY-EIGHT

It came from inside the print works, so I quickly removed my phone and used it as a mirror again. I could see a light go out as a door closed, then I watched a figure hurry across the floor. He got to the back of the building, then climbed some stairs to a door. He opened the door and light flooded out. I could see he was a big man, but moving lightly. An athlete. Perhaps a fighter. He was one of the security detail. I had located my target.

The door closed and the light disappeared.

I stood up and looked through the window. The floor was empty once more. The light was almost non-existent but I could make out the shadows of the giant printing machines. And I knew where the light from the door had been. So I knew where I was going. I opened the door at the end of the corridor and stepped on to the factory floor. Now came the truly dangerous few moments. I had to cross to the door without making the slightest noise, moving through a factory the floor of which was strewn with God knew what. It was an obstacle course and I didn't have the map. So I removed my flashlight and covered it with my hand. Then I switched it on.

Enough light escaped to show me what was directly under my feet. I found a passage between the machines and began walking towards the back of the room. I was lucky; whoever supervised this place insisted on tidiness. There were barrels of oil and ink, and assorted tools, but they were all to the side, leaving a clear path for me. I made my way carefully and soon found the rear exit of the plant. Light from outside seeped in under the door and I had my bearings. I moved cautiously along the door to my left until I got to the end of it. Now I inched along the wall, slowly, making sure not to make a sound. Closer and closer. Then I reached the bottom step. I let a little more light stream out. I could see concrete steps stretching up to a door about three metres above me.

I risked the flashlight. I played it along the wall above me. I was at the side of the plant opposite where the offices had been. There seemed to be a section divided off from the floor, probably a storage area. I could see large double doors, ideal for bringing in and out paper. Above this section there was a second floor that the stairs led to. From the length of the space I guessed there were two rooms. That squared with the information from La Donna; he had some rooms in the back of the plant. Two rooms, two security men and one target. And just little old me to overcome them. These were the moments I lived for.

I took the stairs carefully, sticking to the edges. I got to the top and paused, listening. I could hear nothing. But I knew someone was on the other side of the door. So I took out the tumbler and held it to the thin wood. I applied my ear. It didn't take long. After about thirty seconds of silence I heard a creak and then a sigh.

Bats can pinpoint a sound with startling accuracy. Humans can't. But the sound seemed to be coming from in front of me and to the left. That was my impression. As the door was in front of me, I knew that part was right. To the left was more supposition, but good enough to go on. I considered briefly the best way to approach it. I had one thing going for me, the element of surprise.

The snag with surprise is that it doesn't last long. The bodyguard was sitting inside on a chair – the creak – alert but expecting no trouble. He may have had a gun in his lap, but probably not. It would be holstered under his shoulder, or lying on a table beside his chair. It takes a moment to recover from surprise, perhaps half a second. It takes another moment to get a gun out and into play, perhaps a second and a half. So I had two seconds to subdue the man behind the door. That was what surprise was worth to me, a lousy two seconds. Still, it was better than nothing.

I was determined not to be a target so I would come into the room moving fast. I took out the Baby Browning and cocked the trigger. I should have done that earlier. The click sounded like a crack of thunder. Most modern guns don't need to be cocked but the Baby Browning is old school.

Had he heard the click? I didn't know but, if he had, it reduced my surprise by a considerable amount. I opened the door as I cocked the pistol. The weapon was in my left hand because as soon as I entered the room I threw myself to the right in a dramatic dive.

He moved a lot faster than I expected. I was barely in, just starting my dive, when the first shot rang out and I felt a searing pain in my left upper arm. It felt like someone had branded me with a hot poker, but my arm was still functional. It was a flesh wound.

I managed to get off two shots as I fell towards my right. The Baby Browning is not a very accurate gun but in a confined space, even shooting with my left hand, I was sure of my target. I put one round in his shoulder, the other in his thigh. Two rounds and I had disabled his shooting arm and brought him to the ground.

Except he didn't fall. And his arm was not disabled. It was swivelling towards me, trying to get a bead on my new position. He was wearing jeans and a white t-shirt and I could see no tell-tale rosettes of blood. I had hit him twice and I might as well have been shooting at a ghost.

The bitch.

La Donna had stitched me up. She had given me a gun and I had checked that it was loaded. But I hadn't checked that they were live rounds. I was firing blanks. No matter how good your aim is, if you are shooting nothing you won't hit anything. And if I was firing blanks everything else was a lie. Milosz was not alive. There was no passport waiting for me. And La Donna had set me up. It explained how my movements were so well known by my pursuers and how they had known where they could take a shot at me in the street. I had been played.

My shoulder hit the floor and I bounced and skidded along the carpet. Once I stopped moving he would apply the *coup de grace* and my game was over. So I kept moving. I rolled away from him and tossed the useless gun into the air, aiming at the light. I could see him momentarily lose focus, following the flight of the gun. Then he refocused on me. But it was too late.

The Baby Browning hit the light bulb above our heads, shattering it and plunging the room into darkness. He fired, but I was rolling and his second shot missed me. He should have shot ahead of me because of my roll, but he hadn't. I got to my feet as quickly as possible and two more shots rang out. Both missed in the darkness, but he had the advantage. I didn't know what gun he was using but I assumed he had a full magazine. That could leave him with up to fifteen more free shots at me. The odds were not good.

But the guy was a pro. He stopped firing blind and waited. Eventually I would have to move and any noise would betray my position. He waited. I waited. This was a staring game and I wasn't going to blink first. A minute passed. Two. Five. Damn, he was patient.

Then he spoke. His accent was thick and heavy, but his English passable.

"You have no escape. Just give it up. If you do, I don't have to kill you."

What did he think I was, an amateur? Of course he had to kill me. That was the game. So I said nothing. I waited. Another minute. Two. Not five. Not this time. He broke first. I heard him move. I knew he would. I put myself in his position and I thought it out. He had only one sensible option. If he could get to the door I was trapped. So he was moving towards the door. He was moving quietly, but you can't move completely silently. You will always make some noise. And I don't think he was too worried. He had the gun.

I sensed rather than saw the shadow move across the room. Perhaps I was hearing micro-noises and my brain was interpreting them into a sense of where he was. Perhaps it was telepathy. But I was fairly sure he was in a crouch and moving slowly in a diagonal towards the door. He would pass within about half a metre of me.

I could feel his body heat, smell his sweat and the stink of garlic on his breath. I was right. He was passing right by me. And then he had passed.

That was when I moved.

I stood up and jumped, landing on his back to bring him down with a tackle. I didn't time it quite as well as I hoped, but close enough. Instead of catching him cleanly across the shoulders I was slightly to the side, but I got my right hand hooked around his arm and we both dropped to the floor. He began to spin but I got his back. Now we were locked into a hand to hand battle. All soldiers are trained for it and the way he tried to shift me from him, the moves he used, told me he was ex-army. He had the moves.

I let him spin me on to my back. Now he was on top. But I had both arms around him, pinning his upper arms to his body. Which took his gun out of play. He could only use it if he could free his arm. And I wasn't going to let that happen. He tried to head butt me but I moved my head to the side and he missed me. He kept struggling to free his right arm, as I knew he would. If he had dropped the gun and fought hand to hand he might have beaten me. But he focused too much on the weapon.

I moved my legs up around his waist, hooking my ankles and squeezing. The pressure was on his lower ribs and I was preventing him breathing. He needed to break out from my legs, but he couldn't. I moved my legs up a bit more, increasing the pressure. Soon my ankles were close enough to my hands and I let one of his hands go free. He squirmed, but I reached the fork that was taped to my ankle. Then I released my other hand. Now his gun hand was free. I had to move fast because I knew he would be.

I grabbed his face, feeling, with my left hand. Then I brought the fork up and stabbed viciously for his eye. My first blow went a bit wide, striking the bone around his eye socket. He screamed. My second blow found its target. I could feel the slight resistance, then the tines of the fork went straight into his eye. The goo in his eyeball, the vitreous humour, squirted out and down my hands, making the fork slip from my grip. But the damage was done. He had dropped the gun and stopped struggling. He was screaming. I pushed out from under him and stood up. I reached into my pocket and took out my flashlight. I stood back and took aim, then I kicked him in the head.

He went down. Was he dead? Was he alive? Did I care? I have an ethical thing about collateral damage, but he ceased to be collateral when he had tried to kill me.

I picked up his gun and was straightening up when the door opened and there was a clatter as something was thrown in. Then the door closed.

The gleam of my flashlight picked it up. It was a hand

grenade.

TWENTY-NINE

A grenade is very much a niche weapon. If you encounter one in an empty parking lot, you can lie down three metres away and the blast will spoil your hair do but do very little other damage. But stand up and it might kill you. From fifteen metres away you are safe. Grenades fragment when they explode and the fragments can be lethal. Or they can miss you completely. A hit and miss sort of weapon. But it is different in a small room. You can stand up, lie down or walk around on your hands. It makes no difference. You are dead.

When I saw the grenade roll across the floor and the door being pulled close, I knew I was in trouble.

Hand grenades have a time delay fuse of seven seconds. Pull the pin and throw the thing and it will blow up after a slow count to seven. Which meant that in the early days brave soldiers would pick up the grenade and toss it back. So the time delay was reduced to four seconds. An experienced soldier would pull the pin and count to two before throwing the device, which left very little time to take evasive action. But only a soldier with a death wish would count to three. So that left me a tiny window.

I did the only thing I could. I stepped over the guy I had kicked and ran into the inner room. As I stepped behind the door the grenade exploded. The bang, magnified by the small space, nearly burst my eardrums. I would hear that ringing in my ear for the next ten minutes. But I suffered no other damage. I couldn't say the same for the guy I had left on the floor. I wasn't sure what condition he had been in after I had kicked him in the head, but I knew what condition he was in now. Mincemeat. Well tenderised.

There was a pause of a few seconds, during which the ringing in my ears reduced a little. Then a voice called into the room. The words were in Italian. It's a language I don't speak, but I am vaguely familiar with. I got the gist: *Are you all right?*

If he was so concerned, he might have checked on his colleague before he threw in the grenade, not after. I said nothing, just waited. It wasn't long.

After about a minute I heard the door open and the second man walk into the outer room. I knew what he would do. He would check the body on the floor, to see was it me or his colleague. He had to check.

I counted to three, then stepped into the room with my flashlight. I shone it right at where I knew the body was. The Italian looked up at me. I put a bullet straight through his forehead.

Then I stepped back into the inner room and switched on the light. It was time to assess the damage. My shirt was a write-off. The arm was ripped where the bullet had slashed through the fabric and it was covered in blood. The blood was still flowing freely, but not spurting. That meant no arterial damage. No fear of bleeding out. And there was no exit wound, just a long deep gouge in my arm. It needed stitches, plenty of them. And that wasn't an option right now. So I did the next best thing. I tidied up the arm with a towel and wrapped the wound with duct tape. It was painful as the tape went over the raw wound, but it stemmed the flow of blood. The real pain would come later when someone would have to rip off the tape. Hopefully there would be anaesthetic available, or at least a very large double whiskey.

Finally I ripped the bloody sleeve off my shirt and put the shirt back on.

As I was about to relax there was a crackling hiss from the outer room. Someone was trying to raise one of the bodyguards on his walkie-talkie.

I picked up the walkie-talkie and pressed the receive button. La Donna's voice filled the small room. She spoke in rapid Italian, but again I got the gist. Was I dead?

I hit the transmit button and covered the microphone part with my hand, to distort my voice. In my best imitation of a spaghetti western villain, I said: "Il bastarda e morto."

Even as I threw down the walkie-talkie I knew that *bastarda* was wrong. It's a feminine noun, if the word exists in Italian. But I didn't think she'd be standing outside criticising my diction. I would get away with it. So I checked the gun I had taken from the guy whose eye I had forked. It was a Walther PPK and he immediately went down in my estimation. It's not that it's a bad gun. It's perfectly fine. But owning one is like owning a Porsche 911. It says more about the owner than anything else. The guy was a James Bond wannabe. Now he was dead, like most Bond villains.

The PPK is a semi-automatic and packs a far bigger punch

than my Baby Browning ever could. But it only held eight
rounds. No wonder he hadn't chosen to just fire wildly and
hope to wing me. In my head I went over our encounter.
He had taken four shots at me. And I had shot the second
assassin. So five rounds were gone. I had only three shots left.
But I knew La Donna. She would be on her own. Three would
be enough.

I left the chamber of death with all its carnage and walked
across the floor of the factory. I knew my way now and I
walked fast. I didn't hit anything. I could hear the outer door
open, then the second door, the one with the keypad, opening.
I stood in the shadows and waited. Through the windows I
could see her pass along the corridor. She flicked on a light.
She had no worries.

She opened the door to the print floor and stood there, her
full figure revealed against the back light. She struck a pose and
called: "Guido?"

I should have shot her then and there. Instead, I stepped
forward.

"Why did you betray me?" I asked.

THIRTY

She reacted fast — faster than I expected. Her hand was a blur and she shot at me one-handed. The bullet missed me by a foot and ricocheted madly off the machines around me. I got one shot off and clipped her hand. She dropped her gun. And then she was running.

I pounded up the staircase and set off after her.

When I reached the door she was well ahead of me. She had an advantage of about twenty metres. I had two bullets left. With a full magazine I might have paused and tried a shot. But it was too risky. Could I hit a moving target in the dark with a strange gun? If I could, I would have been the most surprised person there. So I began to run.

She turned right on the street, away from the main road and the town. This was a bit foolish, because lights and people meant safety. But she was still reacting instinctively. She was running into the harbour, into darkness and isolation. So I followed.

You have two options when pursuing someone on foot. The first is to run like the clappers and catch them. The second is to run slowly and keep them in sight. Everyone runs like crazy. Here's why that doesn't work. I am a fit man. I can cover a hundred metres in less than twelve seconds, just. But not without a warm-up, and not in street shoes. La Donna could probably cover it in fifteen seconds. She had a twenty yard lead. I wouldn't catch her in 100 meters. And if I ran that distance flat out I would be knackered. I couldn't maintain that pace and she would escape. So I slowed down and ran hard, but within my comfort zone. I kept the distance between us to twenty metres, allowing her to run herself into exhaustion. I stayed the right side of exhaustion. This way I had some hope of catching her, eventually.

She ran down the road, between where the cruise ship had been half an hour earlier and the blocks of the industrial estate. She passed out of the industrial estate and deeper into the harbour. I followed. The light was less here but there were still plenty of street lamps. A busy port is never completely dark. We ran past small boats, big boats, fishing boats, cargo vessels. She hesitated for a moment, then resumed her headlong flight. That hesitation told me. She had realised her mistake. She was running down a long pier and at the end of the pier there was only water. And behind her was only me. She would need to find concealment or jump on to a boat. But I was too close behind her. So she kept running.

She began to slow and I could see her shoulders shaking. This was a big effort for her and her lungs and heart must be screaming for mercy. Mine were too. I slowed. No point in getting to her too exhausted to do anything.

By the time we reached the end of the pier we were both walking. There were no lights here and the nearest boat was fifty metres away. We were alone. She got to the very edge and could go no further. Like a cornered cat she turned to face me.

"Why?" I asked again. We were standing about three metres

apart. She had her hands on her knees and her breath was coming in heaving gasps.

"For the money, dear. Why else?"

We stood looking at each other, our breathing gradually returning to normal.

"You would have done the same to me," she said.

I doubted it, but I let the remark go.

"Were you against me from the start?"

She shook her head.

"When you walked into the hotel that first night I knew the word was out that you weren't to be helped. But I wasn't going to get in your way. We're friends. We go way back. I was going to slip you what you needed and pretend I had never seen you."

"What changed?"

"I told my boss back in Naples that you were here. I had to do that much. And he sent word back that I could pick up the contract on you."

I sighed.

"How much?"

"A hundred big ones. Someone really wants you dead. I'll get a very big payday when I make that happen."

"If you make that happen."

She shrugged. "If."

Then she said it again: "You'd have done the same."

She looked at my face.

"Maybe you wouldn't have. But baby, that's the game we play."

I said nothing.

"I suppose you shoot me now."

I hadn't thought it out that far. Was I going to shoot her? It's one thing to shoot at someone who is shooting at you. I have no problem with that. I have no problem putting a bullet in the head of a scumbag who has it coming, especially if there is a fat fee lodged to one of my bank accounts. But this was a woman I had known for many years. I had shared good times and bad with her. Could I end it all like this?

"Will you at least permit me a last cigarette?"

I nodded, but held the gun on her.

She moved her hand slowly, reaching for her pocket. Slowly she removed a pack and took out one cigarette. She put it in her mouth and tossed the pack behind her, into the water five metres below us. I heard it splash.

"Do you have a light?" she asked.

I shook my head.

"Of course not. You don't smoke. Mr Goody Two-Shoes."

"They'll kill you," I said.

"Do you think I'll live long enough for that to happen?"

Her hand came down to her pocket, tapping it. No lighter. Her hand moved around to her back. She was smiling at me.

"Found it," she said.

Her hand came back into view slowly. Nice and easy. As it registered on me that she wasn't holding a lighter her hand began to move a hell of a lot quicker. It was coming up to shoulder height, ready for the shot. She was holding a pistol.

I had been lulled into carelessness and my gun was by my

side. I began to bring it up at the same time as she did. She was fractionally ahead of me, so I shot from the hip and aimed low. I squeezed the trigger and felt the recoil against my wrist. The bullet caught her in the knee, which surprised me. That was where I had been aiming. Some shot in the dark in a hurry. I impressed myself.

Her shot rang out wildly, the bullet missing me completely and pinging off the concrete of the pier way behind me. She staggered backwards and fell to the ground. Her gun clattered uselessly away from her.

Her face was pale and strained with the pain. For the first time she looked worried. I think it was finally dawning on her that she would not be picking up the hundred big ones.

"I told you that smoking would kill you," I said.

I stepped forward and placed my foot against her hip and pushed. She was heavier than she looked and she tried to grab my leg with her hand.

"I can't swim," she squealed.

As her hip rolled over the edge she let go my leg and grabbed for the concrete side of the pier. Her hands scrambled desperately but found no purchase. She fell five metres and hit the water with a dull splash.

I looked down. She had hit the water feet first and sunk, but she bobbed up fairly quickly. Her arms flailed wildly and she tried to dig her nails into the sheer wall at the base of the pier. I could see her nails scraping but finding no purchase. Then she went under again. This time she stayed under longer and I could see some bubbles rise to the surface. Her face reappeared. For a moment our eyes locked and she tried to scream at me. It came out in a hoarse rasp: "Fuck you."

Then she sank for the third time.

When I was sure she wasn't going to reappear I turned and walked away.

THIRTY-ONE

It had been a tough night and I needed a whiskey and a hug and I wasn't fussy where they came from or in what order. With no firm plan in mind some instinct drove me to the hotel where Jelly was staying. She had said to look her up in the morning if I was still in Croatia and it was now past midnight. That was technically morning.

The hotel was a small modern one, a good walk away from the old quarter. I got there around four. It was cheap and cheerful, the sort of place popular with backpackers and inter-railers. It would have free wi-fi and a buffet breakfast and few guests over thirty. It also had a door that locked at midnight and a night porter on the reception desk. I could have asked him to buzz me in, but I wasn't a guest so he wouldn't have obliged. Instead, I walked around the back and found a service entrance near the kitchen. It is a little known fact that these doors are used by hotel staff who want to sneak off for a cigarette break and are always unlatched.

I let myself in and walked through the dark and deserted kitchen into the dining room, laid out for the buffet breakfast in a few hours' time. The cereal was already out and so was the fruit, but not the milk or the bread. I grabbed a banana and made like a monkey. I was ravenous. The door from the dining room to the main body of the hotel was unlocked so I walked out into a corridor. Left led to the reception, right further into the hotel. I knew her room number and it was on the other side of the hotel. But I wasn't going to walk through reception. So I went the wrong way, found some stairs, got to an upper floor, walked a maze of corridors and dropped down close enough to her door. I knocked softly.

There was no answer, so I risked a louder knock. I heard sheets being shuffled, so I knocked more insistently.

"What?" came a grumpy and sleepy voice.

"Message for Miss Jenny."

Even with the trauma of the night, I had the wits about me to remember her real name, the name she would have registered under. A real porter would have had her surname as well, but I wagered she was too sleepy to notice the discrepancy.

"Can't it wait until morning?" she grumbled. So I knocked again.

"Okay, I'm coming."

There were sounds from the room as she hastily pulled on some clothes, then the door opened a crack.

Jelly wasn't a make-up sort of girl and she looked gorgeous with her hair all tousled and sleep in her eyes. She was wearing a t-shirt and panties, a good look in a bedroom. It took her a moment to register who was on the other side of the door and a look of something difficult to register crossed her face. Then she smiled.

"Aren't you going to let me in?"

"Isn't it a bit late to be calling on a respectable woman?"

"You said morning. It's after midnight," I explained. "And

I'm hoping you're not respectable."

She opened the door and I stepped in. I pulled the door closed behind me. She faced me.

"It went wrong," she said.

"It went very wrong," I confirmed.

Then I stepped forward and she put her arms around me. At first it was a hug, but then she touched my face and our lips met. Our tongues began to explore, gently teasing, and before I knew it we were moving towards the bed.

I like to think of myself as a Casanova, smooth and gallant in the bedroom. Except all the evidence points the other way. Instead of smoothly laying her down on the bed, I tripped and we fell in an untidy heap, laughing.

But we quickly came together again, our lips and our hands eager. I pushed her back on the bed and she grasped my shoulders, running her fingers down my arms. She hit the duct tape and my whole body tensed.

Then she froze.

"What's this?" she said, struggling to sit up.

"It's nothing," I said, but the mood was destroyed.

She stood to switch on the light and came over to the bed, wincing against the brightness. My arm was a mess. I had no sleeve on my shirt, the skin was red with blood and there were about three layers of tape binding my bicep. But I felt great. I was alive.

"Tell me all about it," she said as she began to look at the mess.

"It's nothing, just a flesh wound. The bullet passed right

through, did no damage."

"Jesus, you were shot and you were going to say nothing."

"I didn't want to worry you."

"Bullshit. You were thinking with your dick."

That too. There was real anger in her voice.

"It went a bit bad," I said. "I was set up. When I went to the location to pick up my new papers, there was a shooter waiting."

I didn't really want to say anything more, but she was glaring at me. Women have a way of looking at a man and making him feel like a boy again. So I went on.

"It's nothing really. There was a bit of a barney, but it all worked out fine. I got away. I don't have any papers, but no harm done."

"Really?"

"But I do have to lie low for a while and I will have to sneak out of town tomorrow evening. But we always had a plan B and I should be able to manage."

She had gone to the bathroom as I was talking and she returned with small nail scissors and a towel. She cut through the tape and pulled it from my arm. Coming off my skin wasn't as bad as I had feared because the blood had made the arm slippery. But it hurt like hell coming off the wound itself. A splurge of blood oozed. But it was old blood, trapped under the tape. The wound seemed to have stopped bleeding.

She did her best to clean it up, then went to her suitcase, which was at the end of the bed, and returned with a bottle of vodka.

"Thanks," I said.

She ignored my outstretched hand and instead of giving me the drink she poured a measure neat on to my torn arm. It felt like a red hot poker had been dragged across the torn skin and it took all my self-control not to scream like a baby. Hopefully any bacteria in the wound were screaming like babies too and shrivelling up.

"You could have warned me."

"You should have figured it out. What else do we have as disinfectant? I can hardly ring reception and ask for a first aid kit. What will I tell them? A strange man is in my room and he's been shot...? Use your noodle."

She was right, so I clenched my teeth and let her get on with it. She made me take off my shirt, which she tore into long strips. She soaked one in vodka and wrapped it around my arm. Then she tied two more strips around it to secure it, using the scissors to trim the ends of the knot. At the end of her ministrations it was stinging but it didn't hurt too much. About the same as if someone had hit it with a baseball bat two or three times. Nothing more. And I could take that.

She sat back to survey her work – and my buff body, I hoped. I am not the best looking guy in the world, but years of training have at least given me the six pack and the broad shoulders.

"What now?" she asked.

"I was hoping you would let me stay here for the night. I have a friend due into the port tomorrow evening and I will sneak on to his boat and he can smuggle me home. That was our plan B."

"Why wasn't it your plan A?"

Good question.

"Because he couldn't get here until tomorrow and guys have been chasing me and shooting at me for a few days now. I thought that speed might be important. A rookie mistake. I should just have found a beautiful woman and hid in her hotel from the start."

She smiled at that, which was a beginning.

"So you just catch the boat and go home? Adventure over."

I sighed.

"The fall-out from tonight might be a problem."

Now the frost was back in her eyes as she looked at me. I had to go on. At this point, honesty (of a sort) was my only card.

"The guy that shot at me ended up a little bit dead," I said.

No point in mentioning his friend and La Donna. If you want to score, you don't want the lady to think of you as a psychopathic spree killer. One body, I could claim self-defence. Three, smacked of carelessness.

She shrugged.

"Casualty of war," she said. God bless her military background. "So there'll be a murder investigation in the town when the body is discovered?"

"The alarm will be raised a little before eight tomorrow and there will be a major kerfuffle, I imagine. And the main exits from the town will be monitored. That includes the port, where my friend is meant to pick me up."

"Shit. Do you have a plan?"

"I do," I said with more confidence than I felt. "I plan on making love to a beautiful woman, knocking back a full tumbler of that vodka and sleeping until noon."

She smiled.

THIRTY-TWO

I thought our first time would be frantic and energetic, a purely physical release. But I was wrong. It was slow and easy and agonisingly intense. I think it was because we were both too tired for the teenage lust phase of the relationship.

Our lips came together, then our hands, then our bodies. I pushed her gently back on the bed, my hand slipping up inside her t-shirt until I was cupping one of her breasts. It was small, but the nipple was hard as a bullet. I began to knead it gently. But then she rolled me over on to my back and got on top.

"Let me do the work," she whispered, biting my ear gently. "You just sit back and enjoy the ride."

I did as I was told. I went to pull off her t-shirt, but she slapped my hand away. She was straddling my body now, leaning down and letting her long hair tease my face. The feathery touch was exquisite. Her hands were running up and down my chest, then she slid down my body, letting her hair trail along my face, my neck, my chest. Her hands were on my belt now, loosening the buckle. I could have helped her but I relaxed and let her do the work. She was in charge.

She slid down to my knees and worked my trousers free of my hips. Then she yanked them off and all that was left were my jocks. One of her fingers hooked the waist and she pulled them down. In army parlance, I sprang to attention. I could feel her long hair gently teasing my groin and then her head bobbed down and she took me in her mouth. I nearly exploded, but she knew what she was doing and she kept me on the brink. Then she slid up my body and our lips locked. She used one hand to guide me in, then wrapped her arms around my neck. Her small breasts pressed against my chest. And her hips began to move in a slow and graceful dance.

Wave after wave of pleasure coursed through my body, but I managed to hold out until I could feel her breath quicken and her movements become more jerky. Then I let myself go.

Afterwards, I didn't get the tumbler of vodka I wanted because almost instantly I fell into a deep and dreamless sleep. I didn't wake until nine the following morning. And I didn't get up until ten. Our second time was as wonderful as the first, but this time I got to be on top.

I came out of the shower at ten-fifteen with a towel wrapped around my waist. I was feeling good aside from the injured arm. The pain was severe, but I could live with it. It was a steady throbbing pain and you can ignore those. Jelly was back in bed. While I had been in the bathroom she had ordered a room service breakfast. There was toast, a grapefruit, a bowl of cornflakes and a pot of coffee. Only one cup, as she hadn't wanted to let reception know she had a non-paying guest in her room. But that wasn't a problem. I went back to the bathroom and returned with the toothbrush glass. I pulled back the covers and joined her in the bed.

She took the grapefruit, I took the cornflakes. We shared the toast. She had a cup of coffee. I had a glass. It felt idyllic.

"What are you going to do?" she asked.

"Phone my man and see what time he expects to arrive. Then make my plans," I said.

While she was in the shower I put the call through to Bill.

"Bad news," I said. "You can't put this trip down on expenses and get the days back."

"Milosz wasn't alive? I half suspected it might be a set-up."

"Pity you didn't share your suspicions with me," I said icily. I gave him the rundown on the night's events.

"Chin up," he said. "The cavalry are riding to the rescue."

"But how do the cavalry pick me up? Every cop in the city will be on alert and a man with his arm bandaged up and no papers is going to arouse some suspicion."

"I can't help you there," he said. "I assumed I would dock at the marina, you'd come on board and we'd sail off into the wide blue yonder. That won't be easy now, but we'll slip you on to the boat somehow. Then Venice. Once you're there you are back in the passport free zone. Our ETA is five so I'll phone you then and we can improvise something."

When Jelly returned to the room I told her a small boat was coming to the marina that evening to pick me up and take me to Venice. Once I was on board, my problems were over. At that point I would begin the hunt for the warlord who had ordered the hit. The best defence is attack and I was going to be his worst nightmare.

Jelly surprised me with her reaction.

"Maybe I can help. I'll come to Venice with you."

Getting no response from me, she went on: "You didn't think this was a one night stand? I'm not that sort of girl. I'm killing time until my brother gets to Europe. I would like to kill it with you. And Venice is on my bucket list."

"How...?" I began.

"Unlike you, I have a passport. So I just go to the marina and join your friend's boat. Having me there might make it easier to slip you on board."

There was no denying the sense in her words. We had the glimmering of a plan.

THIRTY-THREE

I spent the day in the hotel room. Jelly put a Do Not Disturb notice on the door and I relaxed as best I could. She went out for a few hours, returning with chinos, a t-shirt and a white linen jacket for me. Perfect disguise. She also had a pair of leather loafers that I was to wear without socks. I would fit in perfectly with the rich tourists.

More importantly, she had bought disinfectant and fresh bandages from a local pharmacy. It was a painful few minutes, but she cleaned up my arm again and re-bandaged it. Then I put on my new clothes. I felt great, fully relaxed for the first time since I had sat down to meditate in the hostel in Mostar post-assassination. I felt I had passed the crisis point. La Donna had betrayed me but she was dead. Bill was on his way. I merely had to evade the local police – how difficult could that be? – and begin plotting my strike-back.

Jelly had her bag packed and was ready to check out. She was in skinny jeans and a white t-shirt just tight enough to reveal rather than conceal her body. I stood up and kissed her, feeling the old stirring. We had time. Round three – I was doing well and without the chemical aids La Donna had been forced to use to coax a performance out of me.

Jelly responded to my kiss and I could feel her breath quicken.

Then my phone rang.

"No one speaks English in this shithole but Ben has us tied to the dock and some greasy local has said we're good to disembark. The cavalry has arrived, baby!"

We walked out openly, arm in arm. We looked like any other couple enjoying a break. I carried Jelly's bag on my good arm. She offered to carry it herself but I felt that would draw attention to us. We live in a liberated age but if a big man lets a small woman carry her own bag it destroys the illusion of them being a couple.

We took a taxi to the edge of the old town. We got out at a wide plaza where everyone seemed to stop. There is anonymity in numbers.

People were strolling around enjoying the late afternoon sun, oblivious of the drama playing in the background. I could see a few policemen scanning the crowds but that was the only sign that three people had been murdered the previous night. With luck they would put it down to a relic of the war years and be looking for someone local. A gringo like me was unlikely to arouse suspicion.

And it might not be as bad as I thought. La Donna's body could have floated out to sea or be trapped in rocks at the base of the pier. Two bodies in the same location would make for a lesser investigation. Either way, I would have to go with the flow and take my chances when they arose. As I knew they would.

When we got to the harbour it was immediately obvious that things were bad. Very bad. There was an armed checkpoint at the harbour entrance. Beyond that I could see a heavy police presence, including two police vans, outside the print factory. Several rolls of yellow crime scene tape had been liberally unfurled around the building.

We stopped well short of the harbour entrance and stepped into a small café. I picked a table near the rear and ordered two coffees. Jelly left the luggage and went down to the checkpoint to see what she could learn. She came back ten minutes later looking pale.

"You didn't tell me there were two."

I shrugged.

"Technically, I only killed one. The other was killed by his colleague."

"And that makes a difference? You have to be honest with me if you want me to help you."

"Okay – there might be a third body they haven't found yet. But that's it."

"Shit. You didn't tell me your second name was Rambo."

"Your coffee is going cold."

"Don't try to distract me."

"I wouldn't dream of it. But you distract me all the time. You're gorgeous."

She smiled at that, blatant though it was. And I moved swiftly on: "What do they know?"

"They told me that two men were killed in a shoot-out over drugs. Two Italians. There was a trail of blood leading away but they lost it. They believe that the killers got away on a boat in the middle of the night. But they are taking no chances. They are checking everyone going into and out of the harbour."

There goes plan A, I thought. Walk down the marina and hop on board. I hadn't really believed that would work, so I wasn't too disappointed. But I reckoned plan B would be complicated and unpleasant. In the absence of any other idea, I got Bill on the phone. He agreed to come on shore and join us in the café.

Then I went to the toilet. While I was in the cubicle I wiped my gun free of fingerprints, lifted the lid of the cistern and lowered the gun into the water. I replaced the lid. With any luck it would be months before the gun was found. I got back to the table as Bill and his son Ben were walking in. Ben, still a few months shy of seventeen, had grown hugely since I had seen him last and was now five centimetres taller than his father – but still thirty kilos lighter. He grinned when he saw me.

"Hi, Uncle Eli," he called.

I grinned too and we hugged. I wasn't really his uncle but he had called me that since he was knee-high to a small dog. An American thing, I believe. I shook hands with Bill. It was good to be among friends.

"This is Jelly," I explained, introducing them. "She's ex-special forces and is helping me out here."

She raised an eyebrow at that but didn't contradict me.

Bill sat down, waved a waiter over and said: "Three beers and a Coke." Then he turned to Jelly and me.

"Anything for you folks?"

It was good to see that he still couldn't take things too seriously.

Over the beers we discussed everything but the situation facing me. We talked about their boat trip, the sights in Dubrovnik, what we wanted to see in Venice. Finally Ben stood up.

"I know you're in trouble, Uncle Eli. So I'll go for a walk and let you all talk it through. Give me a call, Dad, when you're done."

He shook hands with me, smiled shyly at Jelly and left.

"Lovely kid," said Jelly.

"The best," Bill and I chorused.

Then we got down to brass tacks.

It was obvious that I wasn't going to walk on to the marina and board a boat without arousing suspicions. I had thought I might slip into the water and swim to the yacht, but with the police presence in the harbour area that was not going to work either. I was looking at Jelly for inspiration when I remembered our first date. The Café Buza, where I had dived into the sea. There was a thought.

I outlined my plan and Bill immediately objected.

"I don't like it," he said.

"Of course you don't. You can't swim."

"Got me there. And you can? With an injured arm?"

That was a good point. But I can cover a kilometre in open water with no difficulty. If they could bring the boat close to shore I would only have to do a hundred metres and I could use side-stroke. I didn't really see a difficulty. And no one else had a better plan. By default we agreed to go for it.

"Just be careful of the sharks," said Bill.

THIRTY-FOUR

When Ben rejoined us we had a good dinner, a sort of last supper if things went wrong. I enjoyed every bite of it. I don't know why it is but I find hunger is never affected by danger. And I would need to be fully fuelled up for the evening ahead. Bill and Ben also enjoyed the food but I was not so sure about Jelly. She seemed tense. Bill and I were used to operational problems and Ben didn't really know what was going on. Jelly knew and wasn't in the life. So I suppose it was natural she worried.

We shared a bottle of wine and that kept the conversation flowing.

At eight, they stood up to leave. There were hugs and handshakes all around. Their part of the plan was simple. The three of them would walk back to the marina. Jelly would show her passport at the port authority office and have her bag checked by Customs. Her bag contained some of my stuff, including my phone. She would board with Bill and Ben and they would leave port around nine-thirty. That left them plenty of time to get into position off the diving cliff by ten.

My part of the plan was equally simple but more difficult in execution. I would have to get to the bar unobserved, then dive into the water and swim to the boat. It might be odd to see a man jumping into the water late at night but at least my earlier visit had established me as a diver. I would tell the barman I was doing it for a bet, to amuse my friends on the boat below. It was believable enough.

I set out on foot, taking my time like a real tourist. I stopped and looked in shop windows and lingered in places along the way. I wasn't really loitering. I was checking reflections in the windows and trying to throw followers off their stride. But I spotted no one. I timed it to reach the bar around nine-thirty. The place was still quiet but beginning to fill up. Mostly young people. At one table was a nun of all things, nursing a glass of white wine. The barman recognised me. He grinned and mimed a diving motion with his hands. I gave him a thumbs up.

I should have ordered a coffee but I went for a beer instead. I reckoned the adrenalin would keep me awake and alert without the need for more stimulants.

"You make a dive tonight?" he asked.

"I might do. Some friends have asked me to jump and swim to their boat."

"Then pay your bill first before you dive," one of the locals joked.

I found a table and sat down. I was on the main platform, furthest away from the entrance to the bar. The view was worth paying for. The Adriatic was stretched before me, the sun sinking low in the sky, giving a rosy hue to the wispy clouds. As the sun sank lower the glow intensified. The sun seemed to get bigger before plunging into the water, leaving a bright yellow path twinkling along the calm water.

There were myriad boats on the water, some going, some

coming. But as the sky darkened most began heading towards the marina. One didn't; it was flowing against the others, slowly making its way along the coast. It took about ten minutes from when I first saw it to reach a spot directly out from where I was sitting. It was about four hundred metres off shore as it slowed down. The prow edged towards me and the boat began slowly making its way nearer the shore. There was no way of knowing if it was the right one. It would complicate things if a second boat was in the vicinity.

One of the figures on the deck stood up and draped a white towel over the front railing. That was the signal. I had found my rescue vehicle.

I stood and approached the bar. I ordered a coffee. Now was the time for the caffeine buzz. The barman looked at me oddly as he prepared the espresso. The machine was cold because it hadn't been used for a few hours. But finally the thick pungent liquid dripped into a small glass and he handed it to me.

"It lines the stomach for the beer," I explained.

I settled my bill and returned to my table. The boat was only two hundred metres off shore now. I was feeling confident. The dive itself would hurt because of the wound on my arm. But the shock of the water might numb it. Or the salt might sting like hell. Either way, it was only pain. It was not debilitating.

I let the espresso cool while I continued to sip my beer. I had time yet. It would be a mistake to dive too early and end up in the water for too long. That would draw attention to myself. It was getting nicely dark now. The people in the bar would see me jump, of course. They would probably cheer wildly. But no one else would see me. I would hit the water as a shadow and silently glide to the waiting boat. By dawn, I would be in the middle of the Adriatic and home free.

I finished the beer and put the glass down safely. Then I lifted the espresso and tossed that back. It was bitter and good. I was ready but in no hurry. This was meant to look like a fun stunt by a mad tourist, not a frantic attempt to escape. I looked at the various platforms where the kids had been diving two days earlier. I chose the lowest this time, about ten metres above the water. There was no girl to impress. I pushed my chair back. I was about to stand.

Someone dropped something at one of the neighbouring tables, and I heard a voice: "Mi scusi..."

I looked over and saw the nun had dropped her purse. She pointed to it and I smiled.

"No problem, Sister."

I stood and walked over to her table, dropping down to pick up the purse. As my head dropped below the level of the table I could see one of her legs was out straight and in a heavy splint. And one of her hands rested on her lap. In the hand was a silenced handgun. It was pointed right at my forehead.

I picked up the purse, straightened up and dropped it on the table. I pulled out a chair and sat down facing her.

"Hi, La Donna," I said. "Good to see you."

THIRTY-FIVE

She didn't look pleased to see me. She looked furious. And why not? I had left her for dead less than twenty hours ago.

"Don't Hi me, you fucking prick," she said. "You tried to kill me."

She said it in a low whisper that would not carry to the surrounding tables.

"You tried first," I said. I was trying to keep the tone light but this would seriously hamper my escape. Or prevent it entirely. "You learned to swim?"

Her face turned black.

"I can swim. That was a lie," she snarled. "I was hoping you would throw me in the water."

"And I did. Ever the gentleman, that's me."

"You shot me first."

"I did – but you kind of forced my hand when you drew on me. Was I meant to fall down dead and let you collect the bounty? Look, this is getting us nowhere. You're pissed off at me. I get that. You want to kill me and still collect the bounty. What now?"

"Now I shoot you," she said. "I shoot you in the gut and as you slump over I call for help. And as they try to save your sorry ass, I walk away."

"Hobble away," I contradicted. There was a crutch leaning against the table.

197

"What prevents me screaming my head off and getting you caught?" I went on.

She reached into her purse and removed a small aerosol and placed it on the table between us. I was familiar with it. One puff and I would conveniently pass out, allowing her to put the silenced slug into my gut unopposed.

"I have thought of everything," she said with a smile. She looked me right in the eye. "Yesterday was about money. Today it is personal and I will enjoy it. It is a shame I cannot stay to savour it, but we both know a gut shot is not a nice end."

Her hand reached for the aerosol and her eyes flickered towards it for a second. Nobody reaches for anything without looking. It was not enough of a distraction but it was all I would get. I grabbed the bottom of the table with both my hands and flipped it violently over, throwing it into her face. As her chair began to topple backwards she got off one shot, but it sailed harmlessly into the air. No one noticed that; the slight sound had been masked by the clatter of the falling table. Immediately there was noise in the bar as patrons ran to help straighten her up.

I turned and ran too. Instinct guided me. I ran from the bar and out along the path towards one of the diving platforms. I didn't want to go back in the direction of town. I had to make my dive tonight. Especially now.

As I reached the edge of the diving platform I risked one glance back. She was on her feet, grasping the crutch with one hand. The barman was trying to force her into a chair and she was cursing him. Suddenly I saw a muzzle flash and he hopped on one leg and began swearing loudly. Then he fell over and clutched at what was left of his ankle.

The crowd around Sister La Donna fell away as she waved the gun in a menacing circle, then she began limping towards me, the crutch under one arm. She was moving surprisingly fast, drawing the gun up to take the shot. I could dive, but if she didn't hit me in the air I would be an open target as soon as I hit the water. I crossed the diving platform and followed the path away from the bar. I heard the click click of her following me, the crutch beating out a rapid staccato rhythm against the ground. Her first shot missed, but not by much.. I ran on. I knew the path went further but how far did it snake across the cliff face?

She was still following me. Damn. There were two options and this was the worse of them. It would have been so much easier if she had accepted defeat and tried to make her getaway. I kept running. She was not going to catch me. Unless I ran out of path.

She surprised me by maintaining her pace. She was moving damn near as fast as I was, which meant she was still within shooting range of me. I ran thirty metres along the cliff path, rounded a corner and then...

And then the path ran out.

THIRTY-SIX

I was at a dead end. I could only proceed if I trusted to my abilities as a rock climber. I am actually quite solid on a rock face, but not in loafers with a shredded arm. And even if I had the proper shoes and unblemished limbs I couldn't get very far before she arrived. She would have a leisurely shot at me. Checkmate. The only solution was to make my dive here.

I looked down. Right below me was a big rock, sticking up out of the water with small waves crashing against it. A dive here would result in the sort of concussion that was fatal; a completely staved-in skull. If I ran back around the corner I could land in clear water, but I was running right into her sights.

Going forward was not an option. Going back was not one. Going down was not one. Up? That was daft. And then the click-clack came very close indeed. I knew she was about to round the corner. We were in the endgame and she seemed to have all the good pieces left on the board.

I flattened myself against the wall and waited, holding my breath. I had one thing going for me. She wasn't taking any precautions. When you are the hunter going in for the kill you have to throw caution to the wind. The predator rushes headlong and leaves all thoughts of safety to the prey. She had the gun. She was angry. I was getting away. She would rush headlong around that corner, and I would have only a moment to disarm her. Assuming she did not run right into me with the gun pointing forward. If she did, my game was over.

I waited. I could feel my heart beating, far too fast. I could hear the blood rush through my inner ear. And then she was on me.

She came around the corner with the gun in her left hand, the hand closest to the wall of the cliff. Her right hand held the crutch, which was on the side of the path nearest the sea. I stepped out from the wall and smashed my forearm into hers, pushing the gun to the side, forcing her arm into the wall. She got off one shot that went wildly astray. I kept pressing her arm into the wall with all my strength. But the angle was wrong. She was against the wall, I had my back to the sea. She began to push me. I was stronger than her but she had the wall for leverage. For a moment she almost succeeded in pushing me backwards to my death. But I shifted my feet and bent my knees, pushing back against her strongly. For a second I believed I had her pinned. I could get to her side and swiftly reverse our positions. As long as her back was to the wall she was supported and her injured leg was not a disadvantage to her. But once I turned her, it would be over.

I was starting my move when she brought the crutch up sharply between my legs. Lights flashed before my eyes and my knees turned to jelly as the metal stick caught me full in the testicles. I dropped like a stone, my knees hitting the ground hard. I lost my grip on her gun arm for a second, but found it again, gripping the fabric of her black habit near the wrist. I wrapped my other arm around her knee and held on like a drowning man.

That was what saved me. She threw her weight backwards so that she wouldn't be dragged over the cliff and I managed to hold my position. My eyes were watering.

But the funny thing about a blow to the testicles is that though it hurts like hell, it is rarely a game ender. If you are an experienced fighter you can ride out the sudden shock and deal with the pain afterwards. Just look at any boxer who takes a low blow. They are back in throwing punches quicker than you can blow your nose. In the two or three seconds it took me to recover, she tried to force her gun arm down but I managed to hold her off.

Then I made my move. I made it as explosively as a sprinter coming off the blocks and I committed to it fully. Holding her gun arm, I drove my other hand low between her ankles and up under the long flowing skirt of her robes. I reached towards the small of her back, my elbow hooking her crotch. I drove my shoulder into her stomach and stood and twisted and took three running steps forward, charging back up the path and around the corner from where we had come.

As soon as I rounded the corner I dived from the cliff, my foot pushing from the edge and driving me out into the abyss, springing into emptiness with La Donna over my shoulder in a crude fireman's lift. The ground was gone from beneath me and I was falling... falling. We turned in the air, a clumsy cartwheel. She was now on top and I was underneath. Then I was on top and she was under. I tried to fill my lungs in the second I had. Then I was underneath again and my back struck the water with a blow that drove the breath from my body. And then we were sinking, plunging into the enveloping darkness.

Now she had the advantage. I had taken the blow for her and her shattered knee was no longer a disadvantage in the zero gravity of the water. Her fingers were scratching at my face and then she hit me with the gun and I felt the sharp pain above my eye. We bobbed to the surface and the blood began to flow, mingling with the sea water, blinding me. I grabbed her gun arm with one hand and tried to push her head back under with the other. Her free hand grabbed my testicles and she squeezed. We went under again. I let go of her head and grabbed the gun. I wrenched it from her hand.

Here's a fact about guns. They work perfectly well under water. Most people don't know that. La Donna clearly didn't or she wouldn't have been using hers as a crude club. The bullet is sealed and there is enough oxygen in between the grains of powder for the bullet to be fired on a range, under water or even in the depths of space. But water is eight hundred times denser than air and the bullet quickly loses speed once it leaves the barrel of the gun. Within two metres it has slowed to a standstill and will sink to the bottom. The effective range of a bullet under water is a few centimetres.

I took no chances. I jabbed the barrel of the silencer into her chest, straight between her magnificent breasts. I jabbed hard and as soon as the barrel hit her I pulled the trigger, point blank range. A huge bubble rose between us and flew towards the surface. Her grip on me loosened and she fell away. A plume of darkness welled from her chest like a weird rosette and her eyes were open wide with surprise. A few bubbles escaped her lips and she slowly sank away from me. Permanently.

I let go of the gun and swam for the top, breaking the surface and gasping for air. It was over.

THIRTY-SEVEN

I clung to a rock until I had regained my breath, then pushed off and began to move towards the waiting boat, which I could see bobbing in the darkness about a hundred and fifty metres off. I swam on my right side, with my injured shoulder up out of the water. My right arm moved in powerful sweeps and it only took about five minutes. I had ditched the jacket and the loafers to make the swim easier and it felt good to move through the water under the twinkling eyes of the stars.

When I got to the boat they were ready for me. They had heard the splash of my side-stroke and used a flashlight to pick me out. When I touched the side of the boat, three sets of eager hands reached down and pulled me over the edge. I lay on the deck on my back, looking up at the smiling faces of Bill and Ben and Jelly and feeling an overwhelming sense of relief. Now I could believe it: I had escaped from Mostar.

"Don't just look at me," I said. "Somebody make the boat move."

Ben grinned and stepped away. The deck vibrated and the deep purr of the diesel engine filled the small space. We were on our way.

I sat up and Bill grabbed me under my arms and pulled me to my feet, then guided me towards the small hatch leading to the cabin. I had to stoop and used the steps to climb down. I found myself in a space about three metres long, with a sofa and table at one side and the galley on the other. The sofa pulled out to a double bed and there was a small door at the far end that led to a second room that housed nothing but a double bed and some storage space. There was a chemical toilet in a small cubicle by the hatch. And that was it. Jelly followed me into the inner room.

What followed was not a glorious reunion. I was too exhausted for that and I think she was too worried. She stripped my t-shirt off me and began expertly easing the bandage from my arm. The struggle had reopened the wound and it was oozing black blood. But there didn't seem to be any swelling or other signs of infection. The vodka and the salt water seemed to be taking care of that. She went back into the galley and removed a first aid pack from the press above the stove. She cleaned the wound with an alcohol wipe, which was painful, then reapplied the bandage, which felt fine. I stripped to my jocks and went back on deck to use the open air shower. It was marginally warmer than the sea I had come from and I felt cleaner when I returned down the hatch to towel off and put on fresh clothes. That was one of the advantages of having Jelly come on board ahead of me. She had brought my luggage.

Now I felt human again and I joined the others on deck. Already the lights of Dubrovnik were a distant twinkle. Bill cracked open a can of beer and passed it over to me. He opened one for himself. Jelly had a glass of white wine. He raised the can.

"To a successful escape," he said.

We clinked cans. We touched can to glass with Jelly.

"To a successful escape," I parroted.

"We didn't see the dive," said Bill. "But Jelly told us you cut an impressive figure in the air."

"Not so impressive tonight, " I said. "I had company on the dive."

I told them the story of being confronted by La Donna. I could see Bill was enjoying the tale. Not so Jelly, who had a tight expression on her face.

"I think when we get to Venice I should get the train for Rome," she said. "I don't know how much more of this I can take."

I reached out and took her hand.

"It's over," I said.

"And three people are dead," she pointed out.

That was true. But at least La Donna's death spared me the dilemma of deciding whether or not to shop her to Interpol as the Webcam Killer. In the end I would have done the right thing. But this was simpler. Killing the two assassins she had hired did not weigh on my conscience. They were paid hitmen who had tried to kill me for money and they got their just desserts. Her death weighed more heavily on me. We had been friends, of a sort. I had trusted her. We had bounced uglies with each other – and not just when I was chained to a bed and drugged. We had a history and I didn't like the way it had ended.

What consoled me was that I would have liked her ending even less. She had wanted me dead for a fee. And she was not a good woman, not by any stretch. Pure evil would not be overstating the case. So I could live with her death. Quite easily in fact.

"It's over," Bill echoed. "Tomorrow you can spend the day catching the rays on the deck and by evening we will be in Venice."

He turned to Jelly. "We are very open-minded here and if you want to sunbathe European style, that's not a problem with me."

"Thanks, but I'll pass," she said. "It might be too exciting for Ben."

Bill looked disappointed.

"Shit – I should have learned to sail myself and left him at home."

We had a simple meal of pot noodles – two pots each. Bill can be a bit of a foodie philistine. He couldn't tell fois gras from spam. But after the evening I had had even pot noodles were welcome. I just hoped he had packed some bacon for the morning. After the meal Ben took out his guitar and strummed some stuff I didn't recognise but which his father seemed to take inordinate pride in and which Jelly, who was a few years younger than me, seemed to know. It was a very pleasant evening.

A little after midnight we called it a day. Bill stood up and yawned.

"I'll take the first watch, Dad," said Ben.

I looked at him.

"Nobody is going to get to me in the middle of the ocean,"

I said.

He smiled condescendingly, the way only teens can.

"Uncle Eli, it's a sea, not an ocean. And it's full of other boats, so someone has to steer for the night. I'll do four hours, then Dad will take over for four hours."

"The bastard wouldn't let me get a full night's sleep on the way over," said Bill, but he was smiling at Ben as he said it.

Ben went on: "Jelly, you can take the inner cabin. Eli, Dad and I will take the outer one."

She smiled sweetly at him. The innocence of youth.

THIRTY-EIGHT

Ben needn't have worried; nothing improper went on that night. I was too exhausted. I did lay down on the bed with good intentions, but by the time Jelly was ready I was out cold. I woke about six, when the light streaming in the small cabin window caught my face. We banged the headboard for a few minutes, then I fell asleep again. Not very gallant, but I had been shot at and nearly drowned and Jelly would just have to accept that I would make it up to her in grand romantic gestures once we got to Venice.

When I woke for real, the cabin was empty. I checked the time on my phone and was surprised to see it was nearly eleven. I pulled on my clothes and went out on deck.

"Any bacon?" I asked.

"You missed it," said Bill. "Bacon's for breakfast."

I looked at Jelly. She shook her head. Just as I thought; Bill hadn't packed any proper food.

"There's some energy bars in the galley," he said helpfully.

"I put some fruit there as well," said Ben.

"While you're down there you could bring up a round of coffees," said Jelly. She looked stunning in a dark blue bikini.

I came back up ten minutes later with four mugs of coffee and a banana. I looked around. To the left – port side – was a distant haze on the horizon that might be clouds or might be land. To the right – starboard – was another distant haze on the horizon. Italy and Croatia, or cumulus and stratus? I couldn't tell. Looking forward and backward, I could see only sea. Not a boat in sight.

"Christ, we're in the middle of nowhere," I said, sitting down suddenly. "Do any of you know where we are."

"We're following a course down the middle of the Adriatic towards Venice," said Ben. "Most yachts hug the coast and hop from harbour to harbour. It's a week-long sail. But we are heading direct with no stops and we're not sailing. We are on engine. At ten knots, it will take us a day and a half. We'll arrive tomorrow morning."

I nodded as if I understood.

"So tell me, if we are on engine, what's that big sail doing up?" I asked.

"It helps," he said. "But you have to be a bit careful."

I nodded again. He wasn't buying it.

"Seriously, Uncle Eli. You have to be careful on a sail boat when the sail is up. If I have to tack..."

He saw the blank look on my face.

"If I have to turn the boat with the sail to catch a better wind, I have to tack. That means that the boom -" he pointed to the long horizontal beam at the bottom of the boat - "that's the boom; if that moves it will move very fast. And it could hit you."

"How big a problem is that?"

"It could throw you overboard. If it hits you on the back, you'll be all right. But if it hits you on the head you could be concussed or even unconscious when you hit the water. When the wind catches the sail the boom will whip across the deck very fast. That's why we all wear life jackets on a yacht."

I looked at Jelly. If she was wearing a life jacket, it was a very small one. There was very little room to conceal it in the skimpy bikini. Perhaps her boobs counted as a floatation device. I looked at Bill. What he was wearing looked suspiciously like a Hawaiian shirt over a spare tyre. He was sitting uncomfortably close to the edge and puffing a small cigar. Only Ben had a life jacket on.

"Message received and understood," I said. "So we're stuck here until tomorrow morning?"

"Don't look at me," said Bill. "It's not my fault you can't fly."

I shrugged.

"I can enjoy the view."

I looked lasciviously at Jelly. She blushed slightly but didn't look away.

"I can also get on with a bit of work."

Bill raised an eyebrow.

"I need your laptop," I said. "I am going to start compiling a file on Amel Dugalic. I've never met the dude but he's seriously pissing me off. It's no fun people trying to kill you."

"What sort of internet signal do you think you'll get in the middle of the ocean?"

"The sea," corrected Ben.

"I can use my sat phone as a modem."

"Or you could sunbathe with me and enjoy a romantic sail trip," suggested Jelly.

Or that, I thought. Dugalic could wait. His days were

numbered but he could wait until tomorrow. Maybe even the day after. Maybe even … no. I would take today off, but then the hunted would become the hunter.

It was an uneventful but pleasant day. There is no privacy on a small boat but I was in good company. My mindfulness exercises helped keep the frustration at bay and Jelly's bikini kept the boredom at bay.

In the middle of the afternoon Ben killed the engine for half an hour and we swam from the boat, exulting in the deep blue water. It was quite cold so far from land and a little daunting to know that the sea bed was a full kilometre beneath our kicking feet. But when I thought of La Donna sinking beneath me I lost my appetite for the water and came back on board.

That evening we had two more tubs of pot noodles each. Next time, I would do the shopping.

The Milky Way was out in full glory that night and as we retired Jelly spotted a shooting star.

"Make a wish," she said. "Quick."

Before I could stop myself I said it out loud.

"I wish that once this is all over, you'll stay in my life."

THIRTY-NINE

Bill woke me at eight.

"We're here," he said. "Venice. Conference in the main room in five minutes."

"Do you mind?" said Jelly sleepily, pulling the sheets over her body.

Five minutes later, rubbing the sleep from our eyes, we left the inner bedroom and sat at the small table by the galley. Mugs of coffee were waiting for us and Bill had thoughtfully supplied energy bars. Breakfast of champions.

"Ben is tying up. We're not in the main harbour, but at a marina on the edge of the town. We've taken a berth right at the end, as far away from the marina entrance as we can. It's the most private place we could get. You still have no papers."

I nodded.

"So here's the plan. The nearest American consulate is in Milan. You Brits have an honorary consul in Venice but your nearest real consulate is in Milan as well. So Ben and I will drive there, sort out an emergency passport, and bring it back here. It's three hours each way and say three hours to pull the strings. Can you kids entertain yourselves on your own for nine hours?"

"I think I can come up with some ideas," I said, slapping Jelly playfully on her delicious rump.

"And don't go into town. Without papers you don't leave the

marina," he warned. "In fact, you don't leave the boat."

They were gone half an hour later. A military car was waiting for them. We had nine hours of peace and privacy. I felt Dugalic could wait yet another day.

"Let's go back to bed and not worry about the noise at all," I suggested. So we did.

An hour later we were back on deck, having our second coffee of the morning.

"Do you know what I miss?" Jelly said. "I miss bacon. Bill is a lovely guy, but he's no domestic goddess. If I ever see another pot noodle..."

I laughed.

"Believe it or not, he's better around the house than his ex. It's a wonder Ben survived his childhood."

I looked wistfully beyond the harbour towards the city.

"Do you think we could risk going into town and getting a good breakfast?"

She raised a finger and pointed to the small gate leading from the marina. The gate had an attendant. No papers; no breakfast.

"Cheer up," she said. "I can go into town, pick up some ingredients and be back quickly. What would you like?"

"Bacon and eggs. And milk that isn't in a small plastic tub for my coffee. And some fresh bread. And an English language newspaper."

"Do you want slippers and your pipe too, old man?"

She stood up and stretched.

"Be good while I am gone."

"Yes ma'am."

"Seriously. Do you have anything to protect yourself?"

"Jelly, it's over."

But for the sake of peace we began a quick search of the boat. Bill hadn't brought any weapons. There were some knives in the kitchen, but unless I was attacked by soft butter they wouldn't help me much. I searched for the boat's flare gun but couldn't find one.

"It's probably all right," said Jelly. "I just need time to adjust. It's been very intense and I am not as used to all this as you and Bill. I can't just put it behind me like you can."

"A few hours in a gondola taking in the sights with a hot man by your side will help," I suggested.

She smiled and kissed me. Just then her phone went off.

She looked at the screen and a queer look came over her face.

"It's my brother," she said. "I have to take it."

"Let me talk to him," I said playfully, but she kept the phone. She held it very close to her ear and moved away.

"Give me a moment," she whispered in the earpiece.

She stepped off the boat on to the wooden deck of the marina and walked out of earshot. Fine. I get private. Maybe her brother was a bit of a hard-ass, not good with men his sister dated. Or maybe she wasn't ready to introduce me yet. Or maybe she wasn't going to remain part of my life? Maybe I was over-thinking this. Maybe she just wanted to talk to her brother with no one listening. I sipped my coffee and looked out to sea, symbolically giving her the privacy she wanted.

She came back a few minutes later and seemed to be tense.

"How is your brother?"

"Fine." No elaboration. Her gloom seemed to settle like a cloud over my happiness.

"Is he the jealous type, your brother?" Finally she smiled.

"Family shit," she said. "Nothing important. He is on his way to Rome."

"So you'll be leaving me soon?"

"Maybe that's what's wrong. I don't know if I want to be with you, but I don't want to leave you."

The logic of women can be baffling at times. I made some sympathetic noise and nodded in understanding. There wasn't much I could say. A declaration would be coming on a bit strong. Even a klutz like me got that.

Then she smiled a proper smile, which as usual it lit up the room even though we weren't in a room. We were on deck. If we could capture the light of that smile we could knock a bit off our energy bill, I thought.

"I'll do the groceries. I'll even get your paper. Be back in a while."

I watched her walk down the marina towards the entrance, her long graceful back to me, her hips swaying gently, her buttocks... Maybe I lingered on them a little too much for politeness. But she had her back to me. She couldn't see.

She was stopped at the security gate briefly. At that distance I couldn't make out what was going on, or even see her very clearly, but after a few moments the gate opened and she disappeared. I sighed. The last few days had been frantic.

My world had been turned upside down. It's not as if people hadn't tried to kill me before. It went with the job. But no one had ever targeted me and that was upsetting. I hadn't violated my internal code of conduct, but I had stretched it a bit. And in the midst of all that turmoil a wonderful woman had inserted herself into my life. It was a lot to process. I was sitting there morosely on the deck, gazing at the city in the distance, willing, I suppose, her speedy return. God, I was like a moody teen.

Then my phone snapped me out of it.

"Gerry?"

It was Bill's voice, so I went along with it.

"Hi Bill. Who else would it be but Gerry?" I replied. I tried to put an American twang on my accent in case anyone was eavesdropping. "Any news for me?"

"I'm with the consul now and he has agreed to issue an emergency passport. It's not a full passport. It is only valid for a month. But it will get you back to Boston."

I knew the game he was playing. The CIA maintained a number of false identities ready to press into action when they were needed. Bill was burning one of their precious identities to help me out. Gerry from Boston was now no longer a fiction. The careful work that had gone into preparing the identity was being thrown away on a Brit abroad and could never be used again for an American operative. It was a big favour. Bill would never say it – he might not even think it – but I owed him one.

"And you'll owe me two hundred bucks."

"Shit, Bill," I said in my best Texas drawl. "A passport is only one-forty bucks."

"There's a fee of sixty to rush it through."

"Boy, you told me you had contacts could do this."

"And didn't I do it? Shut up and be grateful."

The phone clicked off.

I laughed. Bill was cloak-and-dagger to the end. He would have loved that little game of charades. I checked the time on the phone. Jelly had been gone longer than I expected. There should have been a grocery store near the marina. Maybe she just needed time to process things. I know I did. But I was getting hungry and hunger always trumps emotion. I thought of ringing her, but that would look a bit needy.

So I sat with my back to the marina, staring out to sea. I let my eyes defocus and took a few deep breaths. I let my eyes close as I focused on my breathing, counting breaths in bunches of ten, not chasing my thoughts, not chasing them away, just watching them come and go.

And then I fell asleep. Will I ever master this mindfulness thing?

FORTY

I don't know how long I had been out, but a noise on the
deck woke me with a bang and I was on my feet and turning
almost before I was fully awake. I came around in a crouch,
to present the smallest possible target and brought my hands
up in the classic boxer's stance. I stepped forward and snarled.
Attack. When in doubt, attack.

Then my brain kicked in and I saw that it was Jelly, back
from her shopping trip.

"A bit edgy there," she said with a grin. "And not as alert as
you should be. You spy types are all pants, no hat. I got right
on to the boat before you even reacted. What if I had had a
knife?"

"I would have died happy, looking into your beautiful eyes."

She laughed.

She was carrying two bags. Both were in large brown paper
bags. I stepped forward and offered to take one from her.

"I'm a modern girl. I can carry my own bags," she said. That
was fine by me. My arm still throbbed, despite her best nursing
efforts. I am an ardent feminist and more so when it saves
me having to put myself out. So I followed her down into the
galley.

She put one bag down on the table and told me to sort it out.
She went towards the inner room with the other bag.

"Are we not going to eat that too?" I asked.

"I should hope not. It's far too expensive to eat. It's a present. For you."

"Can I see?"

She playfully slapped my hand away.

"It's for later."

"Tell me what it is."

"It's a lacy bra and panties set."

I raised an eyebrow.

"How is that a present for me?" I asked.

"Think it through," she said and winked at me. She walked into the inner room. I thought it through. Then I grinned. Roll on bedtime.

She emerged ten minutes later and I had the rashers already frying. I threw in the eggs at the last minute and did them over easy. It is one of the few culinary tips I have picked up from Bill and the eggs taste so much better fried that way. I slid the eggs and rashers off on to two plates and quickly browned a few slices of bread on the frying pan. Yachts may be considered luxurious, but few of them have the luxury of a toaster.

We ate in companionable silence, then I told her that my new name was Gerry and I was glad to meet her. She was delighted with the success of Bill's mission. I think she could finally see that it was over. We had beaten the bad guys and made our escape. There could be a future with me in it if she wanted there to be. I really hoped that she did.

"I'm going to catch a bit of sleep," she said after we had finished. "A fry always makes me sleepy. Why don't you go up on deck and read the paper for a while? I'll be up in an hour."

Sounded great to me. I took my coffee – with proper milk in it – and the newspaper and went up the narrow steps and through the hatch into the sunlight. I found a spot on the deck that faced the sun. I sat down with my coffee by my side and the boat's small transistor radio on the other side. I tuned it into a light classics station and opened the newspaper. She had managed to get hold of the *Sun*, a terrible rag. But it was a familiar terrible rag, full of celebrities I didn't care about, actresses I had not heard of and soccer games I had no interest in. I revelled in the banality of it all. It was a touch of home.

With my stomach full, warm sun on my face, a beautiful woman downstairs and something silly to read, I felt all was right with the world for the first time in a long time. Well, most was right with the world. The sunlight was a bit harsh. So I moved to the other side of the boat, with my back to the sun. Now I could read the paper properly.

I had been in the new position only five minutes when a shadow crossed the deck.

FORTY-ONE

The shadow was moving silently and slowly and I almost missed it. It was behind me and to my right. I caught a fleeting moment of darkness in the corner of my peripheral vision. Enough to fill me with unease. If it was Jelly coming up to join me, she would not have been silent. She would have just walked up to me and sat down.

Sometimes when you are confronted with sudden danger your instincts take over and you react before thinking. That can save your life. It certainly saved mine when my room in Mostar had been bombed. But sometimes instincts can lead you astray. Sometimes a more measured response is called for. I kept reading the paper. Now my eyes were not on the lines of print, but on the shadow that was moving around behind me, drifting further to my right. I was tracking the shadow with my peripheral vision, which is never fully reliable. But if I had just looked, the person behind me would have been alerted immediately. And what if he had a gun?

The bastards – would I ever get away from Dugalic's thugs?

I waited. The shadow came closer. What had I around me that I could press into service as a crude weapon? I rustled the pages slightly and turned a page. This movement was enough to allow me steal a full glimpse of the shadow. I went back to the paper, but now I knew. Someone was a little more than a metre behind me and to my right and that someone was crouched forward, moving stealthily towards me. From the quick glimpse I could not tell whether the shadow had a weapon. If it did, so did the person casting it.

It's not La Donna back for a third go? I shouldn't think things like that. I almost laughed but right now I didn't want to do anything to alert my attacker to the fact that he no longer had the element of surprise.

I rustled the paper a bit more. That was my one help now. I could shift position and be ready to react instantly to the first move without arousing suspicion. He would just see a man reading a paper. What was his weapon? In a marina, however quiet it was at this time of day, he would not want to risk a gunshot. So it was probably a knife. Knife fights are the worst; everyone gets hurt. And normally they are won by the guy who gets the first cut in. Rarely are they won by the guy who didn't bring a knife to the fight. That would be me. I hoped it wasn't a knife.

Then he made his move. I saw the shadow of the hand rise quickly over his head. Probably a knife so. Damn.

I moved quickly. I made no effort to get away from the blow that would come as soon as his hand reached the top of its arc. If he had a knife, his reach would be extended by a number of centimetres and getting away only put me out of striking distance of him. The way to nullify a knife is to get too close to let the assailant use it. So I didn't turn from him. I turned towards my attacker. I came in low and the weapon missed my head and hit me hard on the shoulder. The injured shoulder. And I screamed in agony.

The pain was the first surprise. It wasn't a knife that hit me. It was a blackjack, and a professional one at that. A blackjack is a long leather pouch normally filled with lead shot. If you hit someone on the hand with it you can break bones. Hit someone on the head and it's lights out for the rest of the day, then a headache for a week. A clever plan - cosh me and toss my unconscious body overboard. The autopsy would show I had drowned. Any bruise on my skull would be put down to hitting the side of the boat when I went into the water.

The second surprise was that the blackjack was not being wielded by an unknown assassin. I was stunned to see Jelly crouched in front of me, the vicious cosh in her hand. I didn't have time to process it; the pain in my arm was excruciating and the muscles were dead. I was fighting one-handed.

But Jelly had to try to get her arm back up over her head to slam it down on me again. As she raised her arm I hit her in the chest with my shoulder. She hit the deck hard, then scrambled away. I took the opportunity to regroup.

Jelly scuttled back from me on the open deck and dropped the blackjack.

That was not good for me, because she went for her jacket and came out with a gun. I froze.

Slowly she got to her feet, keeping her distance from me. I was on one side of the deck, she was on the other in a crude shooter's crouch.

"Jelly?" I asked.

"Fuck you," she spat back.

Sometimes our lives are like stuck records, repeating the

same pathetic notes. I asked the same question I had asked La Donna.

"Why?"

And I got the same answer.

"Because I was paid well."

"From the beginning?"

She smirked.

"Think it through," she said. "When you saw me first in Mostar, I was waiting for you to walk past. You weren't meant to see me, but typical man you were thinking with your dick. I could have died when you stopped and said hello. I was the one who planted the bomb and I had to wait until you were inside to activate it."

"Cellphone and a sound-activated detonator?"

"It's worked before," she said defensively.

"So when I saw you at the airport..."

"I was tracking you. And when you came to Dubrovnik, I put another plan into operation."

"You were working with La Donna?"

"She was working with me."

How could I have fallen for it so easily? Perhaps she was right: I had been thinking with my dick.

"So how much am I worth?"

"It doesn't matter anymore, because now it is personal. La Donna was my mentor. She was like a big sister to me."

I could see the rage in her eyes and the raw hatred, and I was hurt.

"Did you ever have any feelings for me?"

"Grow up. I told you when I first saw you that I don't have daddy issues."

"I'm only five years older than you, for Christ's sake."

"And not going to get a day older."

She raised the gun and aimed right at my heart.

I ignored the gun and looked at a spot above her and to her left.

"Just in time, Bill," I said.

It's an old trick and it never works. But it often buys just enough time. Her attention faltered briefly and the gun barrel wavered as she thought for a nanosecond of turning around. It was all that I needed.

I stepped up to the boom, the horizontal beam under the sail. And I pushed it with all my strength. It flew across the deck and caught her squarely under the ribs. She staggered backwards and the gun flew from her hand. I stepped forward and kicked it out of her reach. Then she was on her feet and coming at me. And from her first move, I knew I was in trouble.

I was fighting one-handed. She had two hands and two feet and knew how to use them. I had twenty kilos on her. She had youth and speed on her side. For as long as it lasted, it was a good fight. She opened with a front kick that caught me on the hip and followed with an open palm strike that missed my Adam's apple by a whisker. I countered with a spinning hammer blow that caught her on the side of the head. I felt the dull ache as my hand slammed into the hard bone of her skull.

Then she went for my eyes and I side-stepped the crude clawing blow and kicked her behind the knee. She went down on one leg.

That's when she made the mistake. She went for the gun. I dived on to her back and pinned her. She struggled, her fingers stretching towards the pistol that was agonisingly out of reach. She jerked her body violently and the movement gave her another few centimetres. It is very easy to pin someone but difficult to prevent them from moving entirely. A few more jerks and she might inch across the deck to reach the gun. I grabbed for anything I could use as an impromptu weapon and the first thing my fingers locked on was a length of the anchor chain. I wrapped it around her neck and pulled tight, using it as a garrotte. I strained both ends, pulling back on her neck. Her eyes registered surprise and pain, but nothing else. The chain was too cumbersome to cut off the jugular and choke her out.

So I just wrapped it twice around her neck and dragged her to her feet. Her hands clutched at the chain and I pushed her away from me. She staggered backwards and teetered on the gunwale of the boat. It could have gone either way. For an instant she seemed frozen in time, like a tightrope walker struggling to maintain balance on the high wire. Her fingers clawed at the links around her neck while her body tried to maintain equilibrium. It looked as if she might fall forwards on to the deck. Then I picked up the anchor, which weighed about twenty kilos and I threw it towards her.

Instinctively she threw out her hands to catch it. The anchor caught her in the chest and she toppled backwards, over the gunwale and into the water of the marina.

She hit the water with a splash and sank head first, the weight of the chain around her neck dragging her towards the bottom. The rest of the chain began to cascade over the edge, following her down. I looked over the edge of the boat and saw her panicked face looking at me pleadingly, her eyes wide with fear. A few bubbles rose to the surface.

I reacted without thinking. The anchor chain is always secured to the boat and I stopped its headlong rush. Then I grabbed the chain and began hauling it on board. I took in the slack and began to drag her up from the bottom. The marina was about three metres deep at that point and the chain was heavy enough. But its weight was supported by the density of the water and I managed to pull her towards the surface, the chain still secure around her neck. Her head broke the water and she took a deep, grateful gasp.

She was safe now. The chain was holding her and I was holding the chain. I wrapped it once around my hand to keep it secure, then reached down with my other hand to take hers. To hell with the pain from the wound. I could get her out.

"Hold my hand," I said. "I've got you."

She reached out and our fingers touched. I tightened my grip and began to straighten up, hauling her towards the deck.

Then her other hand came up, flashing silver. She screamed at me and drove the knife hard for my throat. I jerked back and it caught me under the rib, drawing blood. I let go the chain. I let go her hand.

Her scream was cut short as she was pulled beneath the

surface of the sea. This time there were no bubbles.

FORTY-TWO

When Bill and Ben returned I was sitting on the deck, finishing the newspaper. I had bandaged the cut to my abdomen crudely, but it wasn't deep. I would survive. I had all our luggage in three bags by my side.

Bill tossed the passport on my lap.

"Gerry Kaplan, glad to make your acquaintance." He and Ben laughed. "There's an embassy loaner car at the gate and we are good to go. I have a good hotel booked and dinner in a great restaurant."

"I chose it," said Ben. "You know Dad and food."

Bill looked around.

"Where's Jelly? Downstairs?"

I shook my head.

"Long story. But the gist of it is, she won't be joining us. It will have to be a boys' night."

Bill looked at me, his eyes soft with understanding, and said nothing. Ben, less used to the ways of our peculiar world, said: "Don't worry, Uncle Eli. If it's meant to be, she'll be back to you. And if it's not, there's somebody else for you."

Then the three of us stepped off the boat and walked up the marina towards Venice.

Two days later Bill and Ben left me in London. I flew to Edinburgh and took a taxi to the hospital where I lived. The hospital was empty; had been for two years since the funds ran out and construction stopped. Some day it would be finished, equipped and pressed into service. Until then it was unoccupied and the insurance on unoccupied buildings is astronomical. So many buildings like that are occupied by caretakers like me. We get free accommodation and in return we treat the empty properties as our home.

So far I have lived, for periods ranging from four months to two years, in an apartment block in London's East End, the Edinburgh hospital, a factory near Swindon, an insurance office in Marseilles and a villa near Barcelona. And in each of those places, in case of emergency, I have stashed passports and other documents, money and weapons. A shame I had never lived in Croatia. I could have spared myself a lot of pain. And not just the physical pain. When I thought of Jelly, it was not my arm that ached, but my heart.

But home was home and the best place in which to recover. I went through my mail, throwing most of it aside to be dealt with later. One, I opened. It was from my sister. Inside the padded envelope was a DVD, which I put into my laptop. It was her porno.

I have to say it was tasteful. The porno turned out to be a Channel Four documentary on the thriving London burlesque scene. Jane, as a classical dancer, performed in some of the cabaret venues. It is a bit odd seeing your sister in a basque with it all hanging out, but there were strategically placed diamanté pasties to save my blushes. I texted her: "Well done, Sis."

Then I texted my brother. I couldn't help myself: "Shocked.

Don't know how she fitted it all in her mouth."

I smiled for the first time in two days.

Then I began to do some serious research. Strike-back time.

I keyed in the name Amel Dugalic. Nothing came up on Google or Bing. So I went over to the dark side, using a search engine only known to a few of us. My screen filled up with a bewildering series of links. There would be days spent in compiling my file and my plan of action. I clicked on one of the links and a photograph came up. It was a man with a thin face and dark eyes and hair that may once have been a dirty blond but was now darkening with age. The texture of the skin looked rough and he was not smiling. His eyes were set far apart, giving him an intelligent look. But they were hard eyes.

I looked into those eyes and I thought of La Donna, dead. No loss to the world, but she had been a friend. Sort of. I thought of Jelly, dead. She had been no friend in the end, but I would miss her terribly, at least for a few days. I thought of the two Italian mobsters lying mangled in a print factory in Dubrovnik, dead. And I thought of the teenage girl whom I had sprayed with chloroform and photographed. And I thought, sometimes this is a seedy way to make a living.

I thought of all those people and my hand closed into a fist. I extended my index finger, making a mock gun, and I pointed it at the face of Amel Dugalic on the screen.

"I'm coming for you, mate," I said.

EPILOGUE
Four weeks later, Sarajevo

Two black Mercedes cars, top of the range, pulled up in front of a fashionable restaurant in Sarajevo. The windows were tinted. They were also bullet-proof, but this was not obvious to the trendy couples and poseurs on the sidewalk.

Three men, dressed in black with dark glasses, got out of the front car. They went into the restaurant. A moment later, the sign on the door was turned, showing Closed to the world. Relaxed, the three men went from table to table, confiscating the mobile phones of the patrons. The building was in lock-down and incommunicado.

After a few minutes one of the men emerged from the restaurant and nodded to the second car. Immediately the driver got out and opened the rear door. A middle-aged man in a business suit emerged, followed by a stunning blonde in her late twenties. She linked his arm and they walked inside. She looked amazing, like an actress or a catwalk model. In fact she was a very expensive call-girl, quite beyond the price range of most of the diners in the expensive eatery.

Immediately the restaurant manager, looking pale, bustled up and almost bowed before the new arrivals.

"Monsieur Dugalic, what a pleasure, as always."

"No – Mr Smith," said the man, with a slight smile.

"Certainly, sir. Mr Smith, always glad to see you," burbled

the manager, trying to catch up. If the man had wanted to be called Kermit the Frog, that was fine by him. "Can I get you a table? A menu? And for your lady friend?"

The man allowed himself to be led to a table near the edge of the room with a view over the entire dining area. The best table in the establishment. He smiled graciously at the patrons whose meals had been interrupted. Most of them smiled back at him. His three heavies had told them that all their meals were being comped and they would get their phones back as soon as the special guest left. Whether they were happy or not, they knew better than to argue.

Dugalic ordered a fois gras starter, followed by lobster thermidor. The blonde went for a mixed herb salad and a demi portion of vegetarian lasagne. They drank the best champagne with the meal, whether it suited the courses or not. That was not the point: the price tag was.

Before the main course arrived, two women were let into the restaurant by one of the men running security. They were both tall, slim and elegant, like ballerinas, but with racks no respectable dancer ever sported. Dugalic looked at their nipples through the thin material of their dresses and thought he could hang his jacket on them. The two girls went on to the small stage, which normally housed a discrete string quartet during special occasions. Some music came over the speakers and the two girls began to dance. Soon Dugalic didn't have to speculate about the nipples because they were on view to everyone in the room. Some of the male diners were clearly pleased with the way their evening was going; their women folk seemed less happy.

Dugalic was ecstatic. One or both of the dancers would join him in a back room after his meal, if he wasn't too drowsy from the food. And there was blondie, who was his for the night. He was delighted that he had decided to take in some culture and swung by the Sarajevo Jazz Festival. He was delighted his wife had not joined him.

The meal was a great success. There was a happy buzz of conversation from the tables around him. People knew they were in the presence of someone, even if they did not know who, and many smiled his way. He felt like the King of Bosnia, a worthy successor of Stephen Thomasevic, the last king. He had been beheaded in 1463, leaving the vacancy. Blondie was the perfect consort and a wonderful conversationalist: she kept her mouth shut and listened raptly to all his stories, laughing often and at the right places.

No one noticed one of the diners, sitting alone and reading a book, occasionally stealing a glance at the two exotic dancers. He was dressed in a dark suit and had the sort of nondescript face that was easy to lose in a crowd.

After the meal, Dugalic called for the dessert trolley and for more champagne. The two dancers continued to gyrate to the music. No one noticed the nondescript man slip into the toilet and no one saw him open a briefcase. There were no witnesses as he keyed instructions into a remote control console and there was no one there to see him remove a normal wireless telephone handset from the case. When he emerged from the toilet, no one noticed that he was wearing a thin black tie and looked just like a waiter.

Two minutes later the man walked up to Dugalic with the phone in his hand and said: "Gospodine, telefonski poziv za vas."

He had a non-Slav accent but Dugalic took the phone from him and held it to his ear.

Just as he did, there was a loud bang outside the front door of the restaurant and the door shook as a bullet struck it. A second thudded into the wood. Immediately the three bodyguards pulled their guns and opened fire, as everyone dived for cover.

No one noticed the waiter as he walked quietly but quickly towards the kitchen and from there out the back into an alley. He wasn't worried about the shots, because he knew that they came from a remote controlled drone and that they were low-power rounds that would do nothing but spread panic. They would not draw blood. No collateral damage. He knew this, because he was the man in control of the drone.

He spoke into his own cellphone.

"Amel Dugalic?" he said.

"You caught me at a bad time," snapped Dugalic. "Some pricks are shooting at me."

"I know," said the man, who was now walking briskly away from the restaurant. "I am the one doing the shooting."

Dugalic's eyes bulged.

"You fucking prick. We'll kill you. And after that, we'll fuck you over so badly you'll wish you were dead."

Ignoring the logical implausibility of that statement, the

voice on the phone went on: "Did you recognise the waiter?"

"What waiter?" screamed Dugalic.

"The waiter that handed you the phone you are talking on right now."

"Of course not, you fuck. I don't have time for this. Someone's shooting at me."

"That's me, as I explained. I thought you would recognise me. You put a hit on me a few months ago. You hired a whole team to try to kill me."

The penny dropped. Finally.

"Eli Varrick?"

"The same. Two women who meant something to me died because of that contract you put on me. I asked them one question and I'll ask you that question now. Why?"

"Varrick – fuck you."

Eli grinned. He hadn't really expected an answer. He pressed a small button on the remote in his pocket and a radio signal travelled outwards at 300,000 kilometres a second. It was picked up in less than a nanosecond by a small receiver in the handset of the phone that Dugalic held in his hand. The receiver sent a signal to a detonator; which did what detonators do.

It was a small explosive charge, but it was in the earpiece and plenty powerful enough to blow most of Dugalic's head off his shoulders, spraying the wall, the ceiling and nearby diners with blood, brain and bone fragments.

The blonde froze, her pale complexion freckled by the mist of blood. Then a small glob of greyish brain matter slid off her cheek and fell to the crisp white linen table cloth and she screamed.

Eli Barry heard the explosion, muffled by the intervening distance, and he smiled.

It was time to go home.